Loveswept ® 734

HUSBAND WANTED

CHARLOTTE HUGHES

D0041161

BANTAM BOOKS
NEW YORK · TORONTO · LONDON · SYDNEY · AUCKLAND

HUSBAND WANTED

A Bantam Book / April 1995

If you would be interested in receiving protective vinyl covers for your Loveswept books, please write to this address for information:

Loveswept
Bantam Books
P.O. Box 985
Hicksville, NY 11802

ISBN 0-553-44495-6

Published simultaneously in the United States and Canada

Bantam Books are published by Bantam Books, a division of Bantam Doubleday Dell Publishing Group, Inc. Its trademark, consisting of the words "Bantam Books" and the portrayal of a rooster, is Registered in U.S. Patent and Trademark Office and in other countries. Marca Registrada. Bantam Books, 1540 Broadway, New York, New York 10036.

PRINTED IN THE UNITED STATES OF AMERICA

OPM   0 9 8 7 6 5 4 3 2 1

ONE

Fannie Brisbane slathered warm butter onto two pieces of lightly toasted whole wheat bread, cut them into eight perfect squares, and set them on a plate between Gussie and Ernestine Dempsey.

"Thank you, dear," the older sister said. "You always know just how we like it."

Which is why the Dempsey sisters, both in their seventies, walked five blocks for breakfast at the Griddle and Grill each morning and claimed it was the highlight of their day. They enjoyed listening to the latest gossip and having their horoscopes read by a smiling Fannie.

Only today Fannie wasn't smiling. There were dark, half-moon smudges beneath her eyes, making her look older than she was. Her long reddish-blond hair, which she always braided and wore in an elegant crown at the back of her head, hung limp as a horse's tail this morning. She hadn't even bothered with blush or mascara or that mauve eye shadow that set off her green eyes so well. Her uniform, which was usually crisp as a new dollar bill, looked as though it had been put on without the benefit of a good pressing.

"Fannie, honey, what's the matter?" Ernestine Dempsey said, her thin face drawn in concern. "I don't believe I've ever seen you looking so poorly."

"Are you having your monthly, dear?" Gussie asked, taking great care to whisper. Her own face was cherubic and ruddy complected. "We have some tonic water at home that'd fix you up nicely. 'Course, it's nasty stuff. Tastes like turpentine, if you ask me."

Ernestine turned to her sister. "Now, you don't know that, Gus. When's the last time you drank turpentine?"

"I know what's wrong with her," a woman drawled in a syrupy voice. Wilhemena Lightsey got up from her stool at the end of the counter, patted her perfect platinum pageboy, and walked toward them, hips swaying in such a way, it was easy to see why she was, more often than not, the topic of conversation at the Clip Joint Barber Shop just next door.

Wilhemena took a seat next to Gussie and leaned forward. Her polka-dotted slip dress, which exposed more cleavage than was proper at that time of the morning, was set off by a red short-sleeve jacket. The outfit had most likely come from her dress shop across the street. No-body loved clothes like Wilhemena. "I'll bet you stayed up all night watching old movies, didn't you, Fannie?" She looked at the Dempsey sisters. "Last night was double-feature night. A couple of tearjerkers. You know how Fannie goes for that stuff. Next day she mopes around like some-body put a run in her best panty hose."

"That's not it," Fannie said mournfully. She stepped up to the counter and pulled a sheet of folded notebook paper from her apron pocket.

"What's this?" Wilhemena said as she took it from her.

"A letter. Read it." Fannie's bottom lip trem-bled as the woman unfolded it. Ernestine and Gussie leaned closer.

" 'Dear Fannie,' " Wilhemena read aloud. " 'Thank you for answering my last letter. It seems as if I've known you all my life' . . ." She paused and glanced at the signature. "Who's it from?"

Fannie replied in a whisper. "My daughter."

"Your daughter!" Wilhemena's eyes resem-bled two perfect saucers.

Gussie and Ernestine exchanged surprised looks. In a booth nearby, sixty-five-year-old Hyram Bodine glanced up from his breakfast of scrambled egg substitute, dry toast, and black de-caffeinated coffee. A mild heart attack six months ago had forced him to give up his usual fried eggs and hash browns with ham and redeye gravy.

"The one I gave up thirteen years ago," Fannie replied. A stranger walked through the door and sat on the opposite side of the counter. She excused herself to wait on him.

"I remember about the baby," Gussie Dempsey said, leaning closer to Wilhemena. "Fannie was working all day at the mill and sitting up half the night with a sick mother. You know her father walked out on the two of them, the sorry cuss." She shook her head and began tsking. "She wouldn't have been able to take care of a baby. 'Course, folks thought the worst of her at the time. They couldn't see she was doing the poor child a favor."

Wilhemena continued to read. "It says here she wants to visit."

"Oh, my," Gussie declared.

Fannie returned. "Did you read it?"

Wilhemena nodded. "You must be terribly excited."

"Excited?" Fannie exclaimed. "Lord, I'm as low as a gopher hole. She can't come here!"

"Why not?" Gussie asked. "I would think you'd be overjoyed."

Fannie's eyes glistened with tears. "You don't understand. My daughter and I have exchanged a couple of letters. She thinks—" She paused and swallowed. "I've sort of misled her about a few things."

"Misled her?" Gussie said.

Fannie blushed. "Well, you know. I didn't

want her to think I hadn't improved my circumstances over the years."

"Exactly what was it you told her?" Ernestine asked.

Fannie's face grew even redder. "That I'm married to this devastatingly handsome man and we live in this fine house with servants. And that I'm going to college in my spare time."

"Well, the college part is true," Ernestine pointed out, "but I still can't imagine why you lied about the rest."

Fannie sniffed. "You've seen where I live. It's falling apart. Why, it's not worth the powder it'd take to blow it up. And I don't have enough money to do what needs doing."

"What does it matter what kind of house you live in?" Gussie asked. "Your daughter is coming to see *you.*"

"I don't want her to be ashamed of me. Her adoptive parents obviously have money. Her father's a big-shot executive with the State Department, rides around in a black limo. I'm sure Mandy's had the best of everything."

This time Wilhemena spoke. "How could your daughter *possibly* be ashamed of you?" she said as though she hadn't heard a word. "You're working full-time—"

"In a luncheonette making minimum wage."

"And going to school at night, getting your education."

Fannie shook her head. "I'm thirty years old, Wil. Most people have their degrees by now."

"Most people haven't been through what you've been through."

"Don't you *want* to see her?" Gussie asked softly. "Aren't you the least bit curious to see how she turned out?"

"Of course I am, but—"

"How are you going to tell her she can't come?" the woman more or less demanded. "She'll feel like—" She paused as though trying to think of just the right word.

Two fat tears rolled down Fannie's cheek. "Like I'm rejecting her all over again."

"You know you can't do that," Wilhemena said, her own eyes moist. She dabbed the corners with her napkin where the mascara was starting to run. "You could come stay with me," she said. "My place isn't fancy by no means, but you're more than welcome."

"What about the fact that I'm supposed to be married?"

"Your husband could be out of town. That's why you're staying with me. Tell her he's in the navy or something."

"I've already told her he's a successful businessman."

"Excuse me," Hyram Bodine said, startling the women so badly, they jumped.

Fannie glanced up at the distinguished-looking man with silver hair. "Oh, Mr. Bodine, I'm sorry," she said, having forgotten about him completely. "Would you like more coffee?" She started for the coffeepot.

"No coffee," he said. "Just hold on there. I couldn't help overhearing you're in somewhat of a bind."

"Oh, it's nothing," Fannie said, embarrassed that she'd troubled her customers with her personal problems.

"Now, don't interrupt me," he said. "I don't like to be interrupted. Especially when I've come up with a solution."

All four women fell silent.

"Seems to me you need a house," he went on, tucking his thumbs into the waistband of his trousers which, thanks to his diet, were so baggy, they had to be held up by suspenders. He refused to spend the money on new clothes when, as he claimed, there wasn't a dang thing wrong with the ones he had. "I've got a fine place," he went on. "It's much too large for just me and my housekeeper. You'd be more than welcome to use it."

Fannie gazed back in disbelief. Although Hyram was a favorite of hers—always joking and flirting outrageously with her—she didn't quite know how to take his offer.

"*Me* use *your* house?" she said, wondering if his intentions were honorable. After all, it was a known fact he was a womanizer, had been all his life. His poor wife had barely been in the ground six months before he'd married some money-hungry floozy with bright red hair and big breasts. His son had eventually thrown her out, then moved out of the family estate himself. This was all before his father's heart attack, a condition only a handful of people in Culpepper knew about, including Fannie, who'd immediately made alterations to his regular menu. She, like the others, had been sworn to secrecy.

She told herself he was only kidding. "But, Mr. Bodine, you live in a mansion. That's hardly what I had in mind."

"It should impress your daughter. That's what you want, isn't it?"

"Are you saying I should let her think the place is mine?"

"That's the whole idea. Besides, it's only for a few days."

"Ernestine and I will help too," Gussie said after a moment, clearly as surprised as everybody else by Hyram's generosity.

Wilhemena nodded enthusiastically. "You know you can count on me, hon. We wear close to the same size. I'll loan you a few of my best outfits so you'll look like a fine lady."

Fannie stared back at them, thoughts spinning, not knowing what to say. "I don't know," she said, shaking her head from side to side. "I appreciate your offers, but it all sounds so dishonest. It's one thing to lie to somebody in a letter, but it's something else altogether to have to stare your own daughter in the eye and do it."

"You want to see her, don't you?" Hyram said matter-of-factly. "You want her to think you've made a success of yourself?"

"Yes, of course, but—"

"Okay then. When does she wish to visit?"

Fannie was still reeling from his offer and wondering whether to accept. "During spring break. The second week in April. That's—"

"That's barely a week away," Gussie cried.

"It was sort of a spur-of-the-moment thing," Fannie said, feeling as though she might cry again. "She doesn't even know if she can get plane reservations at this point." She shook her head at their shocked looks. "I knew it was hopeless."

"Hogwash," Hyram said. "A week is plenty of time to get things ready. And I can teach you all about being refined. There's nothing to it."

Fannie merely stood there, battling indecision. Finally, she shook her head. "It'll never work," she said. "It's too farfetched. We'll never be able to pull it off." She paused. "Besides, I'm supposed to be happily married, remember? Where on earth am I going to find a husband?"

Clay Bodine took a sip of his black coffee and studied the blueprint in front of him. He'd been trying to get excited about it all morning, but he couldn't. It was a simple two-story frame house with a mere stoop out front and small deck along the back.

He'd built a dozen like it.

Someone knocked on the door, and Clay glanced up as his father stuck his head through. "You got a minute?"

Clay tried to keep his expression neutral. He hadn't seen his father in months. In fact, he'd gone out of his way to avoid him. "What do you want?"

"Just a minute of your time," the older man said, coming into the room. "Your secretary wasn't at her desk so I decided to show myself in." He took a seat in one of the fake leather chairs facing his son.

Clay was thankful his secretary, a cute twenty-three-year-old, was taking a late lunch. His father had a penchant for pretty women and would have embarrassed the poor girl with his blatant flirting. Clay would have had to apologize afterward. It had been that way for as long as he could remember.

"You'll have to make it quick," Clay said. "I've got an appointment in ten minutes." He wondered if he could convince his clients to put a covered porch along the front and sides of the house, or maybe some crown molding in the dining or living room. Anything to give it a little pizzazz.

"This won't take long," Hyram said, trying to make himself comfortable in the straight-back chair. "So, how've you been, Son?"

Clay was in no mood for idle chitchat, especially when it was so obvious his father had something on his mind. "Since I've got clients coming in shortly, why don't we cut the small talk and get right to the reason for your visit," he said.

Hyram clasped his hands together and leaned forward, anchoring his elbows on his knees. "Are you going to be mad at me for the rest of your life?"

"I'm not mad," Clay said, although in all honesty he couldn't think of a better word to describe how he felt toward his father. Maybe disappointed was the word he was looking for.

"You never come by the house. Haven't been by in months now. Not since—" He paused as though trying to count in his mind just how long it had been.

"Not since I threw your second wife out," Clay supplied for him. "Or have you forgotten?"

Hyram held his hands out as though surrendering. "I made a mistake."

"A very costly one."

"I was lonely."

Clay thought of his mother, who'd been lonely all her married life. She had never grown accustomed to her husband's philandering, but good breeding and a lot of patience had allowed her to turn a regal head to it all. She'd simply gone about the business of living her own life and caring for her son. The two of them had been very close.

"Why did you want to see me?" Clay repeated, trying to steer his father to the business at hand. They'd argued enough. All their lives, actually. Now Clay wanted to be left alone.

Hyram shook his head, then sighed heavily as though wondering if he and his son would ever be able to patch things up.

"I hear you applied for a loan at the bank a few days ago," he said. "So you could buy that tract of land north of town."

Clay scowled in response. "So much for confidentiality laws," he muttered, annoyed that his business dealings had reached his father's ears. "Okay, so I applied for a loan. So what?"

"I'd like to loan you the money, interest free."

Clay crossed his arms over his chest and regarded the man with a look of outright suspicion. "Why would you do that?" he asked, knowing how tight with a dollar his father could be. Until his second wife had come along and he'd been only too glad to empty his pockets.

"You're my son. The money belongs to you." When Clay didn't respond, he went on. "Of course, I wouldn't advise you to buy that piece of land you're looking at. Not when I can sell you that property along the river," he added quickly. "As I recall, you've wanted that land since you were fifteen."

Clay gazed back at his father for a full minute without saying anything. "I've tried to buy that land from you three times," he said, clearly stunned. "Each time you turned me down flat. What changed your mind?"

"I don't need it. I was foolish to hang on to it. You know how I get sometimes." He paused. "It's not easy for me to let go of something I've worked for. Your mother accused me of being stingy more than once, if you'll remember."

He remembered. His mother had come from money and tended to take material wealth for granted. The Bodines worked hard for what they had and weren't so quick to part with it. "How much?" Clay asked.

"One dollar."

The younger man gave a snort. "Are you crazy? That land is worth millions."

Hyram shrugged. "Not to me it isn't. I've willed it to you anyway, but I figure there's no sense waiting until I die to let you have it. I'll even help you finance that new development you're talking about. The one where the houses are supposed to resemble historic homes."

"How'd you hear about that?"

"People talk."

"Obviously." Clay studied his father for a

moment, wondering what had brought about the change in him. He'd never been a generous man. Except for once, when the gold digger had moved in and he'd lost his head for a while, hiring a decorator from Atlanta to redo the house, building a pool and tennis court on the property, erecting a massive stable out back.

Clay had just gritted his teeth and said nothing, even when his stepmother had sneaked into his room one night in her nightie and made it plain she didn't harbor any maternal instincts toward him. He'd thrown her out and begun locking his door at night. It wasn't until their accountant showed him what his father had spent that he'd finally put his foot down. He'd very quietly paid the woman off, then driven her to the airport in Savannah, but there was no rectifying the damage between him and his father. Two days later he'd moved out as well. That had been almost eight months ago.

"Why are you doing this?" Clay now asked, pushing the bad memories aside for the time being. He noted for the first time that Hyram had lost weight. Had he been sick? "What do you expect in return?" His father was too shrewd a businessman to hand something over without a fight.

Hyram looked offended. "I've already told you, the land is yours. Everything I have is yours, whether you want it or not. Heavens, most children are only too happy to take from their parents."

"I do pretty well on my own. I don't need your money."

"But you're itching for that land."

"Not if there's a bunch of strings attached."

Hyram sighed heavily. "I've never been able to slip anything past you. I *do* need one small favor." He paused. "Do you remember Fannie Brisbane?"

"Fannie Brisbane?" Clay suddenly had a picture of a high school girl with wild reddish-gold hair who wore her dresses too short. "You mean the girl who got pregnant when she was only sixteen and ended up giving the kid away?"

"That's the one," Hyram said. "She's all grown up now, but she has a serious problem."

Clay gave his dad a knowing look. The man hadn't changed one iota. Another airhead with pretty legs. "And you've offered to come to her rescue," he said dully. "How gallant of you."

"It's not what you think. But, yes, I've offered to help, and that's where you fit in."

Clay leaned back in his chair and listened.

Two days later, Clay Bodine walked into the Griddle and Grill and took a seat at the counter. Fannie, who was studying for an upcoming math exam, almost dropped her book.

"Well, if it isn't Clay Bodine," she said, putting the book aside. "Lord, I haven't seen you in a bunch of Sundays."

"Hello, Fannie," he said stiffly. "You got any coffee back there?"

She nodded, taking in the changes that time had carved into his face. He was still a handsome devil. She'd shared a biology class with him in her junior year, sat right next to him as a matter of fact, and her grades had plunged because she hadn't been able to concentrate on her work. She'd nursed a crush on him ever since.

Fannie poured a cup of coffee and set it before him, hands trembling as much as they had in high school. "I just made it," she said. "You'll have to go straight to Brazil to find any fresher. 'Course, that's a lot of trouble for one cup of coffee. Expensive, too, when you consider the plane fare." She was rambling, something she often did when she was nervous. She closed her mouth and bit her bottom lip as though it were the only way she knew to stop it.

Clay looked at her as if he didn't have the slightest idea what she was talking about. "Thanks," he said, hooking an index finger through the handle and raising the cup to his lips. His hands were big and brown, his fingers long and tapered, nails clean and trimmed neatly.

Then, silence.

"Would you like to see a menu?" Fannie asked at last, deciding he wasn't much of a conversationalist. In a way it was just as well. She had too much on her mind, what with her daughter scheduled to arrive in a few short days and her in a tizzy as to what she was going to do about it.

"I'm not here to eat," Clay said. He took another sip of his coffee, his blue eyes studying her from over the rim of the cup. He set his cup down. "I'll come straight to the point," he said. "I hear you need a husband."

At first she thought she'd misunderstood. Once it sank in, she realized Hyram must've said something about her problem. "You?" she said. It came out sounding like an accusation.

"You got a problem with that?"

"No, of course not," she sputtered. "It's just—" She paused. He really was too handsome for his own good, with that dark hair and blue eyes that could only be described as startling and sexy. Cute as a bug's ear, her mother had said when she'd seen a picture of him in his football uniform in the school annual. He'd been captain of the team as well as class president. Unfortunately, she'd never watched him play football. She'd spent her free time working. And when she'd learned he'd been accepted to Duke University, she'd envied him because it was the same week she had decided to quit school and take a full-time job.

She'd be a nervous wreck if she had to pretend to be married to him. "You just don't look the type," she said.

"What type?"

"The . . . uh . . . marrying type." In fact he looked to be exactly what he was, a confirmed bachelor. She knew there'd been women in his life, but nothing serious had ever come of the relationships. Still, she'd been jealous of those women and wondered what it'd be like to arrive at a party on his arm. Or be kissed by him at the end of the night.

Clay looked back at her for a full minute. He'd forgotten how green her eyes were. Not just your average run-of-the-mill green, but the color of new grass shoots in spring. His gaze fell to her breasts. Her figure was still as good as it had been in high school. She'd developed ahead of the other girls, a fact that had not gone unnoticed by the male population. There'd been speculation as to whether her breasts were real or her bra was padded. Some guys had claimed they had firsthand knowledge. Clay figured they were full of hot air. In all the time he'd known Fannie, she'd never given him a come-on. She'd acted like a lady, despite the rumors, despite the fact that she'd worn the shortest, tightest skirts at Culpepper High.

"This isn't the time to be picky, Fannie," he said, knowing they only had a few days to put a convincing act together. "As I see it, I'm doing you one helluva favor by agreeing to go along with this harebrained scheme in the first place."

He was still as cocky as she remembered. "Why *are* you doing it?" she asked.

"I have my reasons. Besides, it's only for a few days. I can go along with anything for that length of time."

She pondered it. She didn't have to be a rocket scientist to see that he was indeed doing her a favor by agreeing to play the part of her husband. Not only was he one of the few eligible bachelors in town—most men her age were either married or homely as a chicken coop—he was the only man who'd stepped forward to offer his services.

"We don't have long," Fannie said, deciding she was desperate and would have to take what she could get. "I'm moving into your father's house the day after tomorrow."

"I'll be ready by the time the curtain goes up," he said, wondering what it was that had prompted his father to help her. She wasn't at all flashy, a quality his father found hard to resist in women. In fact, she looked as if she belonged in one of those health commercials advertising cereals that tasted like tree bark and pine straw. She wore very little makeup, but there'd been a time when she'd worn gobs of it. He was glad she'd stopped using so much. She had the kind of skin that didn't require it, the kind of skin a man liked to touch.

"We'll need to exchange information about each other," Fannie said after a moment.

He looked suspicious. "What kind of information?"

He was as skittish as a long-tailed cat in a room full of rockers, she decided. No wonder he'd managed to stay single all these years. "Just general stuff. Such as birthdays, favorite colors, what you like to eat. If we're supposed to be married, we should know these things about each other."

Clay decided it made sense. "Okay, when?"

"The sooner the better. I have a class right after work. I could meet you at eight o'clock this evening."

"Your place?"

She hesitated. She wasn't proud of where she lived, but it wasn't as if she had anything to prove to him. She only cared what her daughter thought. "That's fine. Should I give you my address?"

"I know where you live," he said, remembering what had been scrawled on the wall of the boys' bathroom with a Magic Marker. *For a good time, see Fannie Brisbane, 11 Appletree Lane.* She obviously hadn't had a phone at the time. He'd borrowed paint remover from his shop class and taken it off, then wondered why he'd cared one way or the other. Maybe his reasons had been self-serving. His father showed little respect for women. He was determined not to be like him.

Clay slid off the stool, grabbed a dollar bill from his pocket, and laid it on the counter. He paused at the door. "I understand you've been writing to your daughter." She nodded. "What'd you tell her about us?"

Fannie blushed even before she said it. "That we were crazy about each other."

TWO

He wasn't going to show.

Fannie checked the old-fashioned clock on the mantel and saw that it was approaching eight-thirty. Clay Bodine had obviously changed his mind about participating in her little charade. Not that she blamed him. Anybody with half a brain could see that it was a cockamamy scheme.

She sighed heavily. It's what she deserved after having lied so shamelessly to Mandy. Now, she had a choice. She could come clean with the girl or think of a reason to keep her from coming to Culpepper.

There was one other option. She could pack her bags and sneak out of town in the middle of the night, before folks found out what a dang fool thing she'd done. But her personal business would be all over town by then. News such as that traveled like stink on a skunk.

Of course, leaving would make her a coward. Sort of like her father, who'd hightailed it out of there as soon as the doctor had diagnosed his wife with multiple sclerosis. He'd caught the first train, claiming he couldn't stand the thought of her being snatched away from him. Ironically, she'd lived with the illness almost fifteen years before it took its toll.

Fannie sighed and glanced around the small sitting room with its outdated wallpaper and threadbare carpet. If only she could afford slip-covers for the furniture, something bright and cheerful to hide the drab greens and browns that made the place look so dismal. Perhaps if she bought a few house plants.

She knew she couldn't afford it. She was barely able to pay utilities and school costs what with all the hospital and doctor bills left over from her mother's illness. The house would have to wait.

She tried to imagine what the place would look like through a young girl's eyes, especially someone who'd been raised in an affluent house-hold.

Her heart sank at the thought. Oh, Mandy, what will you think of me? she asked silently.

Fannie jumped when she heard a car pull into the driveway. She hurried to the door and opened it, just as Clay Bodine climbed out of a bright red Corvette. He made his way up the sidewalk, then paused briefly at the front steps when he saw her. "What's wrong?" he asked, noting the frightened-rabbit look on her face.

"I thought you'd changed your mind," she said. She opened the door wide enough to admit him.

He crossed the sagging front porch and entered the house. "I told you I'd be here. I'm running late, that's all." She'd changed out of her waitress uniform and now wore jeans and a baggy T-shirt. She had obviously taken a shower recently, since her hair was damp. She'd clamped it to the nape of her neck with a wide barrette. Once again, she wore no makeup. She wasn't out to impress him, he realized, and that struck him as odd since most women worked hard at it. He decided he liked that quality in Fannie.

"I don't suppose you have a cold beer on hand?" he said, glancing away when he suddenly realized he was staring.

Fannie smiled. "As a matter of fact, I do." She closed the door behind him. "I stopped by the store on the way home from school. Follow me."

"What's with the floor?" he said, noting how it slanted sharply to one side.

"The house is sinking. I need to have this area jacked up, but that costs money." She shrugged and crossed the room.

Clay followed her and found himself in a paneled kitchen with rough-hewn cabinets that looked as though they'd been built from ply board. The moss-green linoleum floor was badly worn in places and curled away from the wall in others where the glue had long since evaporated.

"Now you can see why I don't want to bring my daughter here," Fannie said, watching him study his surroundings and knowing he was wondering how she could stand to live in such a place. "I've been trying to sell it since my mother died, but once folks see how much work it needs—" She paused and shrugged. "Nobody wants the headache." She laughed suddenly, finding humor in her situation. "I'd burn it down if I had someplace else to go."

Clay was tempted to tell her he wouldn't blame her if she took a match to it, but he didn't. It was still her home. "I suppose we should get started," he said, wanting to get the meeting over with. He'd thought once or twice about canceling. The whole idea—them trying to fool her daughter into thinking they were happily married—*was* the most ridiculous thing he'd ever heard of. But he *couldn't* cancel on her. Not when she only had a few days to get ready. Not when he'd already committed himself. Not when he found that he was looking forward to spending time with her.

"Have a seat at the table," Fannie told him, grabbing two bottles of beer from the refrigerator.

Clay watched her hurry about the crude kitchen, taking two jelly glasses down from a cabinet, pouring pretzels into a chipped bowl. She set them on the table and joined him a minute later with two yellow legal pads and pencils. She handed him one.

"What's this for?"

"For you to write down information about me. Why don't we start with birth dates," she suggested. "I was born June third, nineteen sixty-five."

"January seventh, same year," he said.

They each wrote down the information.

"Okay, my favorite color is green," she told him.

"Red for me."

She smiled. "Which explains why you drive a red sports car." He didn't reply. She mentally shrugged and jotted down the information. "Were you born and raised here in Culpepper?"

"Yeah, were you?"

"Heavens no. I've lived all over. I was born in a place no bigger than a football field called Brady, Georgia. If you spit too hard, you'd hit somebody in the next town."

He looked at her, wondering what to make of her sense of humor. "Yeah, that's small," he agreed finally.

They went on for another ten or fifteen minutes. Finally, Clay paused and took a sip of his beer. "I'm supposed to memorize all this before your daughter hits town?" he said, indicating his notes.

"That's the general idea."

He shook his head. The whole thing sounded absurd, and he couldn't imagine his father going along with it. Of course, men sometimes did stupid things where women were concerned, and his father had proven that fact more than once.

"Why don't you just tell your daughter the truth?" he asked, knowing it would save them all a whole lot of trouble.

One hand flew to her chest as though she were afraid her heart would leap out at the suggestion. "I can't tell her the truth," she said. "Not after all the lies I've told her."

"Maybe you shouldn't have lied in the first place."

She looked at him for a moment. "You wouldn't understand," she said. After all, he was Hyram Bodine's son and had never wanted for anything. He'd never been forced to shop for shoes at secondhand stores, never had to wear his clothes until they were embarrassingly small or had holes in them. He'd never had to be ashamed of what he did or didn't have.

"Try me."

"I already have one strike against me where my daughter is concerned," she said matter-of-factly. "I gave her up. I allowed perfect strangers to raise her."

"So why'd you do it?" he asked, his curiosity getting the best of him.

She gazed back at him, wondering if he had

any idea how much it hurt to hear that question, even after all these years. He had already judged her as a bad person for giving up her baby. And she didn't have the time or inclination to try and change his opinion.

"Look, I don't know how your father got you to agree to this whole thing, but if you want to call it off, I'll understand. There's still time for me to find someone else." She sounded more confident than she felt. Time was running out on her. Mandy's parents had managed to secure a plane ticket, and the girl would be there before she knew it. Still, Fannie wasn't about to give him the satisfaction of knowing how desperate she was.

Clay saw that she was already formulating a plan in her mind as to where to look for his replacement. The thought disappointed him somehow.

"I never back out once I've agreed to do something," he said at last. "You have a problem, and it seems I can help. I may not agree with the way you're trying to work it out, but that doesn't mean I won't go along with it." He picked up the legal pad. "Do you have brothers or sisters?" he asked, continuing with the questions.

"No."

"And your father? Do you know where he is?"

She supposed it was common knowledge that

he'd deserted the family. "I don't know, and I don't care."

He nodded. Any man who'd walk out on his kid and sick wife wasn't much of a man, as far as he was concerned. "So you quit school and went to work once he . . . disappeared?"

"I had no choice," she said sharply, thinking he was criticizing the fact that she'd dropped out of high school. "I've since earned my G.E.D., though, and I'm taking close to a full load at the community college."

"Stop being so defensive," he said, noting the two red splotches on her cheeks and the unblemished skin. He assumed it was due to a strict diet of vegetables. She'd claimed, as far back as high school, that she was a vegetarian, although he'd suspected the family simply couldn't afford to buy meat. Her father hadn't kept a job more than a few months when he'd lived there. "I wasn't criticizing you for quitting school," he said. "I was only trying to get the facts."

She relaxed. "Sorry."

He hesitated before returning to the questions about her child. "What can you tell me about the circumstances surrounding your daughter's birth?" When she looked uneasy, he went on. "In case it comes up."

Fannie sighed and toyed with her pencil. Of course he had to know. Just in case. It didn't matter if he agreed with her choices or not. "I was sixteen years old, working the day shift at the mill. I met a boy." She paused. "We couldn't date like a normal couple because of my mother being sick and all, but he came out to the house from time to time. I guess it simply happened." She paused once more and looked uncomfortable.

"You never considered getting married?"

She met his gaze. "He left town as soon as he found out about the baby."

"I see." Just like her father, he thought.

"Anyway, I started wearing my mother's old dresses. I was able to keep my pregnancy a secret for almost six months."

"Did your mother know?"

"Once I got big she knew. I think she would have gone after the boy if she'd had the strength. But mostly we concentrated on hiding it from my boss at the mill. I couldn't afford to lose my job. He eventually found out, of course. I think he *would've* fired me if several of his best girls hadn't threatened to quit on him."

She smiled fondly at the memory of the women who'd been like older sisters to her. "I don't know what I would have done without them. Anyway, I had about a month to go when one of the women suggested I talk to her minister about finding a home for the baby. And that was that," she added, deciding not to tell him how painful the ordeal had been, how many nights she'd cried herself to sleep. He would never understand what it was like giving birth to a baby and having it snatched away before she could see it. He would think she was mentally unstable if she told him how, later, she'd had no desire to live. If her mother hadn't needed her so desperately, she didn't know what would have happened to her.

Clay put down his pencil and took a long swallow of beer. "What do you hope to accomplish out of this?" he said at last.

Her eyes misted. "I just want to see her. Touch her. I want to be able to go to bed at night and know I did the right thing by sending her away. This may be my only chance."

"Why is that?"

"Her adoptive father is an important man in Washington. He's been offered a job in some country I've never even heard of. Who knows how long they'll be gone. I may never see Mandy again."

"Mandy? That's her name?"

She smiled. "I named her Amanda after my grandmother, and her adoptive parents kept it. Everybody calls her Mandy."

Clay leaned back in his chair. "So you're going to move into my father's house and pretend it's yours so you can impress your daughter?"

Fannie shifted in her seat. She didn't have to be a mind reader to know he thought the whole thing ridiculous. "I really didn't need such a fine house. I just wanted someplace nice. So she wouldn't be ashamed of me."

He was quiet for a moment, his mind moving in another direction. "I suppose that means I'll have to move back home for a few days," he said, although he wasn't thrilled at the prospect. He couldn't help but wonder if that was why his father had gotten him involved. Hyram had tried several times to get Clay to move back, but he had refused.

"You know we'll be expected to share the same bedroom," he said smoothly and without expression.

Fannie snapped her head up and met his look. His ice-blue eyes were sharp and assessing, clear and observant. Nevertheless, she didn't have a clue as to what he was thinking. "I hadn't thought of that."

"We're supposed to be married. And crazy about each other." He paused thoughtfully. "I'm not so sure my father will approve of us sleeping in the same bed," he said, then waited for her reaction.

Fannie hesitated. She couldn't imagine Hyram disagreeing with any of her plans when he'd made it plain he'd go to any lengths to help her. "I'm prepared to do whatever is necessary to make my daughter's visit a success," she said. "That's how important this is to me. Your father will simply have to trust me."

Clay shifted in his chair and pondered it. Experience had proven his father could be gullible where women were concerned. Yet, Clay didn't miss the determined look in Fannie's eyes. She would go to great lengths to see that her plan worked. What had happened to the subdued girl he'd sat next to in biology, the one he'd felt compelled to protect? Had she been hardened by work and adversity?

"We should probably get back to work," Fannie said, realizing they were wasting precious time discussing Hyram Bodine when they needed to talk about each other. "Is there anything else you want to know about me?"

Clay glanced up quickly and was tempted to say, "Yes, I want to know what makes you smile, what lights up your green eyes." But he didn't. "I can't think of anything."

She saw the look on his face and wondered if he was having more doubts. "You don't think we're going to be able to pull this off, do you?"

"How are you going to prevent someone from spilling the beans?"

"I'll have to make sure Mandy doesn't talk to anyone other than those directly involved in what we're doing."

"She's not going to want to stay cooped up in the house the whole time she's here."

"We can take her to Charleston or Savannah. I don't know anyone there. As you said, it's only for a few days."

"You've got it all figured out, haven't you?"

"I guess when you want something bad enough, you do what you have to do."

He considered the remark carefully. It struck him how right she was. He'd agreed to the charade because he wanted that land his father owned.

For some reason the thought made him uneasy.

THREE

The Bodine mansion was an English-style residence flanked by elaborate gardens and a perfect lawn. As Fannie parked her old car next to Hyram's Mercedes, she decided the feed-and-seed business had served him well. Gussie and Ernestine had described his first store as a small lean-to next to Barnard's Service Station on Main Street. After a profitable marriage to a young but rather plain-faced English girl, he was able to build impressive stores throughout the Southeast.

Fannie climbed out of her car and made her way up a front walk of miniature cobblestones that reminded her of the historic district in Charleston. She felt underdressed in slacks and a cotton blouse and wondered all over again if she was making a grave mistake in what she was about to do. What on earth made her think she could pull it off, and why had she gotten these nice people involved?

She knocked on the door and waited, but there was no answer. She had convinced herself to turn around and leave when an elderly woman appeared. She was frail and birdlike, but carried herself regally.

"You must be Miss Brisbane," she said in an accent that was unlike anything Fannie had ever heard. It sounded German, but the words were soft and slurred around the edges, hinting of years spent in the South. "Mr. Bodine is expecting you." She backed away, unsmiling, so Fannie could pass through.

Fannie stepped inside an enormous entrance hall, which was dominated by a freestanding Georgian-style staircase. An antique library table stood along one wall, above which hung an oil painting of several young girls walking down a dirt road, wearing long skirts and frilly hair bonnets. She imagined it was an expensive piece of art. She thought of the bare walls at home and of her mother who'd always liked pretty things but had never had them. Fannie'd had to go out and buy something nice to bury her in.

"I'm Gerta Straus, Mr. Bodine's housekeeper," the woman said, interrupting her thoughts. "Would you come this way, please?"

Fannie followed her into a living room that was decorated like something out of a magazine. The ivory Berber carpet and rose-colored damask upholstery smacked of money. Hyram saw her and stood.

"Welcome to my home, Fannie," he said, holding his hands out and greeting her as if she were a long-lost relative. "I was half afraid you'd changed your mind."

"I was tempted once or twice," she confessed with a shy smile. She discovered her own hands were trembling as she put them in his. "You have a lovely place, Mr. Bodine," she said, noting the elaborate window treatments that adorned the floor-to-ceiling windows and tied everything together. She regretted now that she'd allowed Clay Bodine in her home.

He waved off the remark. It was obvious he didn't spend a lot of time thinking about what he had or didn't have these days. He'd admitted, shortly after his heart attack, that he wasn't as concerned with wealth as he'd once been. "Please sit down. Gerta, would you bring us coffee?"

The housekeeper started for the door. "If I can get His Holiness to let me into the kitchen," she muttered in that strange accent as she disappeared into the hall.

Hyram shook his head, a small smile tugging one corner of his mouth and convincing Fannie he'd been extremely handsome in his day. Not that he was hard on the eyes now, especially since he'd started taking care of himself. All that fresh air and exercise, not to mention the new diet, had softened the age lines around his mouth and eyes.

It was obvious where Clay had gotten his good looks.

"Don't mind Gerta," he said. "She's upset with the new chef."

"New chef?"

"I borrowed him and a young maid from a couple who are leaving on holiday tomorrow. We can't have your daughter eating Gerta's cooking and scrubbing her own bathtub now, can we?" He chuckled.

"Oh, I wish you hadn't gone to so much trouble," Fannie began.

"Nonsense. Besides, it'll be a treat having a real chef for a while. Do you know, he had to drive to Savannah to find the ingredients he needed to stock the kitchen. Claims our stores in Culpepper are pathetic."

"I hope you haven't forgotten about your health problems," she almost whispered.

He paused and glanced toward the door. "I gave him a copy of my diet and asked him to cut fat wherever he could. I trust you haven't said anything to Clay."

"Of course not."

He looked relieved. "Gerta knows I'll cut her tongue out if she breathes a word of it to the boy."

"Why is it so important that he not know?"

He shot another glance at the door. "It's no secret that he and I have had our differences. I don't want him to think his old man is about to kick off and should be pitied. I hope you don't mind, but that coffee will take a while," he said, changing the subject abruptly. "She's as slow as the day is long. And eaten up with arthritis. I keep telling her she needs to retire. She's a proud woman, though. Doesn't like to think she's getting old. So, you found the place all right?" He had to stop to catch his breath.

Fannie couldn't help but wonder how long it had been since Hyram had had anyone to talk to. He hadn't stopped chattering since she'd walked through the door. She knew the heart attack had forced him to retire early, but surely he got out with friends.

"Everybody knows where the Bodines live," she said. "It's the nicest house in town."

"You're very kind. I built this place for my wife, you know. She was raised in England. I hired an English architect to copy the house she'd been brought up in."

"How romantic," Fannie said. "You must've loved her very much." She regretted the words the instant she said them, and she tried to hide her embarrassment. It was a well-known fact that Hyram had cheated on his wife like a dog when she was alive.

He nodded after a moment. "I *did* love her," he said, "although there are some people who would claim otherwise. I thought I'd lose my mind when she died. She was perfectly fine one minute, and the next thing I knew she was dead from an aneurysm." He sighed. "Nothing much seemed important after that, not even the business. I wish I'd spent less time worrying about those damn stores and more time with my family while I had the chance."

Fannie nodded sympathetically. "I know what it's like to lose someone dear to you. After my mother developed complications with her disease, I hated leaving her to go to work. I never knew if she'd still be alive when I got home."

"Life is full of difficult choices," Hyram said, then looked up as his housekeeper came through the doorway with a tray. "Aw, here's our coffee now," he said in obvious surprise. "That didn't take long."

They made small talk while Gerta poured the hot liquid, holding the handle of the pot with fingers that were bent and twisted with arthritis.

"Mister Clay called and said he was going to be a few minutes late, but that he would be here in plenty of time for dinner."

Hyram looked pleased. "Thank you, Gerta. That will be all."

She started for the door, her back ramrod stiff. She paused in the doorway. "I told that new chef of yours I'm not cleaning up after him. You should see what a mess he's made of the kitchen."

"Very well," Hyram said, as though he were accustomed to smoothing his housekeeper's ruffled feathers. "I'll see that it's cleaned properly."

Fannie waited until they were alone to speak. "I'm sorry for the friction between your staff," she said. "This is all my fault."

He set his cup down. "Don't be ridiculous. It was my idea to hire these people in the first place."

"Yes, but you did it because of me. I never meant to put you out."

He waved the comment aside. "Listen to me, young lady," he said. "You may not know it, but you've done me an enormous favor by using my house to entertain your daughter."

"I have?" Fannie asked, although she couldn't imagine how.

"Do you have any idea how long my son and I have been estranged? Eight months now," he said. "I couldn't even convince him to have dinner with me before this came up. Now he's going to be staying here for a few days. Who knows, he may decide to move back permanently, if we can put our differences behind us."

Fannie knew what had caused the rift between father and son; in fact, the whole town knew, but she didn't say anything. "Is that what you want?" she said instead. "For Clay to move back home?"

Hyram nodded. "This house is too big for just me and Gerta. It's lonely too. I'm hoping Clay and I can finally make peace with each other." He paused and smiled. "So you see, you're helping me as much as I am you."

"That makes me feel a little better."

"So tell me what you've heard from your daughter."

"Well, she was able to get last-minute plane reservations. Her adoptive mother wrote me a brief letter and told me right up front that she was struggling with her decision to let Mandy come. I take it both parents are hurt that she decided to look for me, and they're only going along with it because of Mandy's persistence. I didn't write back because I got the impression they wanted nothing to do with me. I'll send them a note of thanks after Mandy's visit."

"It sounds as if you're doing a good job of handling an awkward situation," he said.

"Anyway, Mandy is flying into Savannah airport late Friday afternoon. She has to go back to Washington on Monday, so we only have to . . . uh . . . *pretend* for two and a half days."

"Are you nervous?"

"I'm a regular train wreck, what do you mean am I nervous!"

"Clay will go with you to pick her up. Believe it or not, he can be very comforting at times."

"I hate to put him to the trouble."

"He's already agreed to it. I've never known him to back out of a commitment. Except for a couple of marriage engagements," he added with a chuckle. "But that was different. He claims he was pressured into it by women more interested in a prestigious address than a husband and children." Hyram drained the rest of his coffee and stood. "I suppose you'll want to get settled now. Do you have any bags?"

"Only a couple of small ones. I can bring them in."

"Nonsense! You're the mistress of the house now, someone else can do it. Let me have Gerta show you where you'll be sleeping." He called the woman, and she appeared instantly.

"Would you show Miss Brisbane to her room?" He glanced at Fannie quickly. "We'll have to call you Mrs. Bodine now that you're supposed to be married to my son, but we can work out the details over dinner tonight. By the way, we dress up a little in the evening. Will that be a problem for you?"

Fannie shook her head. "I don't think so. Wilhemena Lightsey is dropping by later with a few things for me to try on. I hope that's okay."

"It's your house now," Hyram told her. "You may do as you wish. In the meantime, I'll send up your things."

Fannie turned for the door. "By the way, what should I call you?" she asked, knowing she couldn't continue to call him Mr. Bodine.

"Call me Hyram. Or Dad. Just don't call me late for dinner." He chuckled softly as though he'd personally conceived the witty reply.

"Okay, Hyram," she said, testing it out and deciding she was more comfortable with it than with Dad.

"I'll show you to your room now," Gerta said, already moving toward the door. She led Fannie up the massive staircase and down a thickly carpeted hallway. "This used to be Mrs. Bodine's room," the woman said, opening a door into a bedroom and sitting area done in cream and white. The sofa and chair, which faced a tiled fireplace, were skirted and adorned with plump throw pillows that gave the room a cozy, slightly feminine look.

"It's lovely," Fannie whispered, noting the elegant, hand-embroidered cutwork spread that draped the four-poster mahogany bed. "I feel guilty using it."

Gerta went to a window and pulled the drapes wide to admit the late-afternoon sunshine. "It's a shame to let such a pretty room sit empty," she said. She paused and walked to the other side of the room, moving so smoothly, one would have thought she was on roller skates. "The bathroom is through there. I trust you'll find everything you need." She paused and waited.

Fannie waited as well, then wondered what it was they were waiting for. "Am I supposed to tip you?" she asked, already opening her purse.

"Certainly not."

"Are you sure? I stopped by the bank and got a roll of quarters just in case."

"I'm positive." The woman moved for the door, head high, back and shoulders stiff.

Fannie followed. "I've offended you, haven't I?" she said quickly. "I'm sorry, I didn't mean to. I just don't know about . . . these things."

The woman paused with her hand on the doorknob and regarded her for a moment. The lines around her mouth relaxed. "I'll show you what I can before the child arrives." She left without another word.

Fannie simply stood there, cocooned in luxury, wondering how she was ever going to blunder her way through the next few days.

"Oh my heavens!"

Wilhemena Lightsey followed Fannie up the grand staircase and into her bedroom and almost dropped the garment bags she carried. "Would you get a load of this place?" she said.

"Nice, isn't it?" Fannie said, draping another garment bag across the back of one chair and wondering how Wilhemena managed to keep her dress shop stocked when she chose to keep so many things for herself. Behind her, a pretty maid carried in several bags as well. She laid them across the settee and excused herself quietly.

"Nice isn't quite the word I was looking for," Wilhemena said. She dumped her own bags on the bed and went into the bathroom where a massive Jacuzzi was surrounded by mirrors and tropical plants. "You've even got a sitting room in your bathroom, for Pete's sake," she called out. "And a heated towel rack. And a telephone. Oh, what I wouldn't give for a place like this." She came out of the bathroom and found Fannie standing beside the window, looking out at the gardens, her expression miserable.

"What's wrong?" she said. "Why do I get the impression I'm the only one thrilled to be here?"

Fannie turned to her. "This whole thing has gotten out of hand."

"What do you mean?"

Fannie sighed heavily, walked over to one of the chairs, and sat down. "This is what happens when you tell one little white lie. You have to keep lying in order to back it up. Before long, it snowballs, and it's impossible to remember all the lies you've actually told." She shook her head. "And now, I've had to drag a bunch of innocent people into it—"

"Those people wouldn't have helped unless they wanted to," Wilhemena interrupted. "Stop beating yourself up."

"I'll never be able to get three days off at the Griddle and Grill," Fannie said, moving to another subject. "I'll have to call in sick. Another lie."

"So what? You've never called in sick in all the time you've worked there. I'll vouch for you, if your boss asks. So will Gussie and Ernestine."

"That's not the only problem, Wilhemena," Fannie said. "Look at me. My daughter will take one look and know I'm not the fine lady I'm supposed to be. She'll know I lied."

Wilhemena waved the statement aside. "That's why I'm here. Before I owned a dress shop I was a hairdresser. Before that, a cosmetologist. When I get through with you, your own mother wouldn't recognize you." She paused as if she suddenly realized how insensitive her remark was. "Sorry, I didn't mean to bring up your poor mother."

"That's okay," Fannie told her. Actually, she was glad her mother wasn't there to see the mess she'd gotten herself into.

Wilhemena went to one of the bags and unzipped it. "Okay, take off your clothes."

Fannie arched one brow. "I beg your pardon?"

"Get undressed," she said. "You've got about three dozen outfits to try on."

Shaking her head doubtfully, Fannie stepped out of her slacks as Wilhemena pulled an array of casual dresses from one of the bags. From another she produced a half-dozen after-five dresses.

"How can you afford all these clothes?" Fannie asked, standing in her bra and underwear.

"I don't pay full price," Wilhemena said, then stopped speaking abruptly when she saw Fannie in her unmentionables. "Oh, that's sad," she said, tsking and shaking her head.

Fannie blushed and tried to cover herself. "What do you mean?"

"You've got a knockout figure, and you wear that old-lady underwear?"

"Cotton is cheap."

"Cheap isn't always better," the woman told her. "Not when it comes to lingerie. But don't worry. We've got time to pick up a few things before your daughter arrives. Here, try this on. We'll start with casual wear first." She held up a linen blend walking short suit and a blue chambray button-down blouse. "Each outfit comes with earrings and panty hose," she said as Fannie stepped into the baggy knee shorts. "You don't want to ruin the effect with the wrong color hose or scarf."

"Uh, right." Fannie wondered what Wilhemena would think if she saw the clothes she knocked around the house in.

"I chose conservative styles for you," she said, using the tone she saved for customers. "While we want you to look slightly sexy, it's still important to dress like a lady."

Fannie nodded as though it all made sense, then checked her reflection in the mirror. "Hey, this doesn't look half bad. How much does something like this cost?"

"Off the rack, about one hundred and fifty dollars."

"Ouch. That's more than my utilities cost in a month."

"Lucky for me I don't buy off the rack," Wilhemena said smugly.

By the time Fannie had tried on everything in the garment bags, she was exhausted. Wilhemena decided what she should wear when and where and hung them in a closet accordingly. She even attached notes stating which accessories went with each outfit. There was also an elegant nightgown, several slips to consider, not to mention shoes. Wilhemena wore a half size larger, but that was rectified by stuffing tissue in the toes of each pair.

"Now we have to do something about your hair and makeup," the other woman said, grabbing a small suitcase. "Come on, there's a vanity in the bathroom."

Once Wilhemena had pulled Fannie's hair free from its braids, she brushed it. "You have nice thick hair," she said. "Why do you wear it up all the time?"

"I have to wear it up at the luncheonette."

"Well, you don't once you get home." She paused. "When's the last time you had it trimmed?" she said, studying the split ends the way a scientist might study a new strain of influenza.

"Back in third grade." Fannie laughed at the look her friend shot her. "I don't know. A couple of years, I suppose."

Wilhemena wet down Fannie's hair with a

spray bottle, pulled out a pair of barber's scissors and got busy. Finally, she surveyed her work. "I know what'd look good on you." She brushed the hair back from Fannie's face and attached combs to each side, then let the hair fall in natural heavy waves down her back.

"You've got gorgeous hair, kiddo, but at your age you don't need to wear it so close to your face."

Fannie looked amused. "At my age?"

"You're thirty, not nineteen. Pull it back like this, and you'll take ten years off."

"Ten years. Wow! Can you pull it back any farther than that?"

Wilhemena chuckled. "Sorry, your ears are in the way. Now, do you own *any* makeup?"

"Of course I own makeup," Fannie said indignantly. "I'll show you, it's in my purse."

Wilhemena groaned. "If you can carry it around in your purse it must not be much. Sit still and I'll show you what a little of it in all the right places can do."

Fannie leaned away from her. "I don't want it caked on," she said, remembering how she'd looked in high school. To this day, she shuddered every time she looked at her old yearbook. If only there'd been somebody to show her how to use it.

"Give me more credit than that, will you?" Wilhemena said.

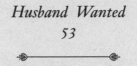

Clay climbed out of his car and slipped on his jacket as he made his way to the front door of the house he'd grown up in. He was late. His appointment had kept him over, then he'd had to run home, shower, and slip into a suit. He thought it dumb to go to so much trouble for one lousy dinner, but his mother had insisted on the family dressing up, and they'd continued the tradition after her death.

Clay paused at the door, not knowing whether to knock or go in. Gerta saved him the trouble of deciding by opening it before he had a chance to do either.

"I thought I heard you pull up." She smiled, something she didn't do often.

"Hey, Gertie, how ya' doing?" She offered her cheek, but he leaned close and kissed her on the lips instead.

The woman sniffed. "I've had better days," she said, opening the door wide for him. "Your father went and hired himself a chef."

"No kidding?"

"And a cute parlor maid to boot."

"Hmm. How cute?" He grinned at the look she shot him.

"Don't get fresh with me, boy," she said. "You're not too old for me to take over my knee."

"Only if you promise to wear something in leather." She pursed her lips at him.

"Hello, Son," Hyram said, stepping into the hall. "I see you made it." He smiled in such a way it was obvious he was pleased about something.

"Sorry I'm late," Clay told the man as they shook hands. "I was held up."

"No problem, you still have time for a cocktail before dinner. Gerta, would you tell Jean-Paul we're all here now?"

Gerta mumbled something under her breath as she made her way toward the kitchen.

Hyram chuckled. "She missed her nap today," he said. "Been grouchy as a bear."

Clay noted the pleasant expression on his father's face. "What's up? You look as if you just got a hot tip on the stock market."

Hyram motioned for him to follow. "Come on, I'll show you."

Intrigued, Clay followed him through the foyer and into the living room. Sitting on the sofa, wearing a black silk crepe de chine suit, was a striking woman with the longest legs he'd ever seen. Clay glanced at his father questioningly.

"I think you've met Miss Brisbane," Hyram said, going to the woman and holding out his hand. She took it and rose gracefully.

It was one of those drumroll kind of moments.

Clay could only stare at her. "Fannie?" He

stepped closer. Of course it was her. Only different. *Much* different. She smiled, drawing attention to full lips that had been painted the color of
ripe strawberries. They looked wet. Wet and inviting, he thought, and felt something tickle his
stomach.

"What do you think?" Hyram said.

Clay shook his head, not knowing what to say
or do next. Her hair tumbled down her back and
shoulders in fat rowdy curls that made him wonder what it would look like against her bare skin.
He realized he was gaping. "You look wonderful," he managed.

"And every inch a lady," Hyram pointed out.

Fannie offered them both a nervous laugh. "I
feel like the sow's ear trying to pass myself off as
a silk purse."

Hyram shook his head. "Nonsense. You're
very lovely. Don't let anyone try to convince you
otherwise. Your daughter will be proud of you."

Clay felt a jolt in the pit of his stomach, right
where the tickling sensation had been only a moment before. His father couldn't keep his eyes off
the woman. "Can I fix anybody a drink?" he
asked, making his way to the wet bar.

"Nothing for me," Fannie said.

"I've got one," Hyram told him, holding up a
glass. "By the way, guess what the new chef is
preparing for our appetizer?" he asked. "Escargots. How's that for fancy cooking?"

"Escargots?" Fannie said, a frown marring her brow. "Isn't that—?"

"Snails," Clay told her, pouring scotch into a glass. He shot her a curious look. "You ever eaten them?" Of course she hadn't.

Fannie glanced from one to the other. She'd heard people ate snails, but she didn't know a soul in Culpepper who did. "N-no, I haven't," she sputtered. "I've stepped on a few in my time, though." She forced herself to smile as Hyram chuckled.

"Don't worry," Clay told her smoothly and with just a hint of sarcasm. "Now that my father has taken you under his wing, he'll see to it that you're introduced to life's finest."

"That's right," Hyram said, giving her a hearty wink.

"Uh, maybe I'll have that drink after all," Fannie told Clay, hoping the snails would slide down easier if she had something to relax her. "Do you have any white wine?"

"Sure." He put his drink down and opened a small refrigerator where several wine bottles were stored. He pulled one out, checked the label, and opened it with a corkscrew that had been placed nearby for convenience sake. He carried the glass to her, and she raised one perfectly manicured hand to take it. "It's a very good wine," he said. "Nothing but the best for the new mistress, right, Dad?"

Hyram raised his own drink. "Welcome to

our home, Fannie. I hope you'll be very happy here." He didn't see the look Clay shot him.

Dinner was tense for several reasons. First, Clay had not sat down in the family dining room in more than eight months, and the strain between him and his father was noticeable, despite all they did to appear civil to each other.

Fannie felt the tension in her shoulder muscles. And then there were those snails to contend with. She watched as Clay, using a miniature fork, pulled the meat from the shell and placed it on a toast point. She did the same, took a big bite, and chewed only long enough to get it down.

"What do you think?" Clay asked, noting the trouble she'd gone to in order to keep from actually tasting the delicacy.

"I think one is more than enough," she said, taking a long drink of water in hopes of washing the garlicky taste from her mouth. She turned to his father. "Hyram, you're welcome to mine if you want them." She was so eager to get rid of them, she didn't bother to ask if they were on his diet.

"I love snails," the older man said, taking her plate. "Thanks, hon."

Clay watched the display with mounting anger. *Hon?* Just what did his father have in mind?

Finally, he shoved his chair from the table. "I think I'll get another scotch."

Fannie saw the pained expression on Hyram's face as his son stalked from the room. She covered his hand with hers. "Give it time. You knew it wasn't going to be easy."

The rest of the meal was delicious. There was a cold avocado soup that Fannie discovered wasn't half bad, a nice salad with Bibb lettuce and a special peppercorn dressing. The main course consisted of duckling in orange sauce with new potatoes and fresh steamed asparagus. Once again, she watched the men for direction.

"You're doing fine, Fannie," Hyram told her, smiling warmly.

Clay, now on his third scotch, had lost interest in his food. His attention remained fixed on the exchange between his father and the young woman. He shrugged mentally and drained his glass. Oh well, why should *he* care if there was anything going on between the two? He was tired of trying to keep his father from looking foolish, more tired still of trying to save the family fortune.

"Do you always go to this much trouble at dinner?" Fannie asked.

"My late wife insisted on it," Hyram said. "She claimed it was the only way she knew to get the whole family together."

"Frankly, I would have a hard time getting used to all this fuss," she confessed. "Especially with my schedule. I hate to admit it, but there are times when I'm so worn-out, I grab a bowl of cereal before bed. Tacky, isn't it?"

"My dear, nobody could describe you as being tacky. Indeed, you are like a rose among thorns."

Clay set his glass on the table with a loud thunk and started to get up, just as the new maid entered. Hyram beamed in her direction.

"Tell Jean-Paul dinner was excellent," he said, "and if he's ever interested in coming to work for me, I'll double his salary." He paused and shoved his chair from the table. "Never mind, I'll tell him myself. Excuse me," he said, nodding to Clay and Fannie. He and the maid disappeared through the doorway.

Fannie shifted in her chair uneasily.

"Your father's very kind," she said when the silence became unbearable and she could stand his penetrable gaze no more. "Not many people would open their homes the way he has for me."

Clay regarded her. "Yeah, he's a real knight-in-shining-armor. I'm sure he has his reasons, though. He usually does."

"What makes you think he isn't doing it out of the kindness of his heart?" she asked, wishing Clay could see the goodness in his father as she did. No matter how selfish and insensitive he'd been in the past, the heart attack had changed everything.

"My father never does anything unless it benefits him somehow."

"How could he possibly benefit from having *me* here?"

Clay leaned back in his chair. "We both know the answer to that, Fannie. Let's don't pretend otherwise."

She stared back at him for a minute. He obviously suspected his father was using the situation to get him to move back home. "You agreed to the whole thing. Maybe you're ready to make peace as well."

He shook his head. "Making peace had nothing to do with my agreeing to go along with this charade. I'm doing it because—" He paused. "Because I knew you were desperate," he said.

"I see." It annoyed her that he felt he had to help her because she couldn't get another man to pose as her husband—and it hurt a little too. She pushed her chair from the table and tossed her napkin beside her plate.

"Well, as you said before, it's only for a few days. Surely we can tolerate each other for that length of time. But don't worry, I'll do my best to keep it quiet. I'd hate for folks in town to find out you had to pretend to be married to plain old Fannie Brisbane." She saw him frown and move his chair from the table as well. "Why, you'd be the laughingstock." She turned for the door.

He reached out and grasped her wrist, bringing her to a halt. "Wait a minute, Fannie. That's not what I meant at all," he said, realizing the scotch had loosened his tongue and twisted his meaning. Which explained why he didn't often drink.

"Isn't it?" she said, realizing, much to her horror, that she had tears in her eyes. "Tell me, how did your father get you to agree to the whole thing? What did he offer you? A million dollars?"

She said it so flippantly, he thought. She didn't have the slightest idea how close to the truth she was. "Look, I'll admit I wasn't looking forward to it. How do you think I feel watching the two of you together?" He regretted it the minute he said it. Once again, his true feelings had seeped through the veneer of control he'd hidden behind for so long.

Fannie didn't understand at first. Then it hit her. He was jealous of the easygoing relationship she had with his father, jealous because the two of them couldn't spend five minutes in the same room without making it uncomfortable for everybody else. "It's your own fault, Clay. Your father is begging for your love, but you won't even give a little. Can't you see how lonely he is? Don't you see how much he needs someone in his life right now?" She closed her mouth and bit her bottom lip. Oh, how she longed to tell him just how close he'd come to losing the man.

Clay stared back at her for a moment. What kind of nonsense was she telling him? That his father had turned to her because his son refused to have anything to do with him? None of it made sense. But neither did the rest of it. "And you think you're the person to take my place?" he asked, trying to understand. "Forgive me, but you hardly fit the role."

Her eyes flooded with tears and spilled down her cheeks. She swiped at them angrily. "I'm not trying to take your place," she insisted. "But I can't help caring about the man," she said. "He accepted me from the very beginning. He didn't try to judge me by my past or the fact that most folks considered my family white trash."

"I know how the boys made fun of me," she went on, "of the clothes I wore. I couldn't have cared less." It was a lie. She *had* cared, but there wasn't anything she could do about it. If her dresses were too tight, it was because she had simply grown out of them in the two or three years she'd been forced to wear them. If they were too short, it was because her mother had let the hems out as far as she could. Of course she cared. But there hadn't been a damn thing she could do about it. Somehow, keeping her mother alive and working to keep a roof over their heads was more important than making a fashion statement.

Clay realized he was gritting his back teeth. It surprised him that he should feel sorry for her, but he did. "I never *once* made fun of you," he said, reaching for her napkin and handing it to her so she could mop her eyes. She was literally sobbing, and he was glad there was no one to witness it. "Come on," he said, prodding her toward the foyer and out the front door. "Let's take a walk. It's time you and I got a few things straight."

FOUR

Fannie was only vaguely aware she was being led to an area of hedges and flower beds. She thought she smelled gardenia. Clay nudged her in the direction of a concrete bench, and she sat down. "I'm sorry," she sputtered. "I can't believe I fell apart." The tears continued to stream down her face as she spoke. "I guess I'm under a lot of stress, what with my daughter coming and all."

"It's okay." He sat there for a moment, quietly, waiting for the tears to subside. Finally, she seemed more in control. "Like I said, Fannie. I never made fun of you. And I never considered you white trash." He remembered the rumors he'd heard about her and wondered about them. Why had she been singled out by the guys? "I know you had it rough," he said at last. "I wish I'd been a better friend in those days," he added, then reminded himself he hadn't been a friend at all. In fact, he didn't remember Fannie having any friends.

She shrugged and wiped her eyes. "It wasn't as bad as all that. There were good times as well. Anyway, I like to think it made me a better person."

He studied her closely. "Some people are hardened by adversity."

"Maybe determined is a better word," she said, thinking of the hospital and funeral bills she still owed but was determined to pay off once and for all by the time she completed her education. One day, when she had a good job and income, she would be debt free. Then she'd be able to make repairs to her house. She'd buy meat at the grocery store, *fresh* meat, not the kind that had been marked down because it was brown. She'd never again wear those ugly cotton panties that had sent Wilhemena into a tizzy.

Clay saw that her mind was at work, and he would have given anything to know what she was thinking. "A penny for your thoughts," he said.

She sighed wistfully as she noted the elaborate garden surrounding them and thought of her own yard where nothing but crabgrass seemed to grow. "I was thinking about how one day my life is going to be different than it is now."

"Different?"

"Easier, maybe." She looked at him. "And, yes, I'm determined to see it happen," she said, knowing she wasn't the least bit afraid of hard work. "I'll do whatever it takes."

Clay listened and wondered if she was counting on his father to help her realize those dreams.

"Now, in my day, we went to a lot of trouble when the family entertained," Gerta said, lining silverware on either side of an expensive-looking dinner plate. "But all that fuss required a battery of servants, and servants are oftentimes more trouble than they're worth. Mr. Bodine got rid of everybody after the missus died, simply because he didn't want the headache of keeping up with them. The new Mrs. Bodine hired a few when she moved in, but, of course, none of that lasted for very long." She waved the whole incident aside as though it held about as much significance as the price of pistachio nuts in western Asia.

"Besides, what does he need with a slew of servants anyway? He never entertains. You're the first overnight guest we've had since—" She paused. "Well, since Mr. Clay threw the second Mrs. Bodine out," she added on a whisper.

"He actually threw her out?" Fannie said, deciding the story sounded more interesting than trying to learn which piece of silver was to be used when.

Gerta shot her a haughty look. "It's bad manners to gossip about one's employer, Miss Brisbane," she said, her tone as crisp as the linen handkerchief tucked into the pocket of her blue-and-white seersucker jacket. She was the model of propriety, gray hair pinned back with nary a strand out of place. Nondescript beige pumps adorned her narrow feet, and her thin legs were encased in thick support stockings.

She drew herself up and cleared her throat as though what she was about to say would give Fannie the insight and wisdom she needed to make it in this life and the next one as well. "Now, you'll note, forks to the left of your plate, knives and spoons to the right, lined up in order of use. Handles in a straight line, approximately one inch from the table's edge." She measured it with a simple wooden ruler and smiled to find it perfect.

Fannie tried to hide her embarrassment at being called down by the housekeeper a moment before. "I'm sorry for prying," she said. "We talk about our boss at the luncheonette behind his back all the time."

"Yes, well, that was before you asked me to teach you how to act like a lady," Gerta pointed out. Finally, she sighed. "But I may as well tell you, for your own good if nothing else, the whole affair with the second wife left a bad taste in Mr. Clay's mouth. He thinks all women are nothing but a bunch of gold-digging fortune hunters."

"No kidding?"

"He'd never admit it, of course, not even to

me, but that boy thinks if a woman looks at him twice, she's wondering about his bank account."

"How sad," Fannie said, thinking of the darkly handsome man with wide shoulders. "I would imagine Clay Bodine would be a good catch with or without his money."

"I guess after watching that female manipulate his father all those months, he figured women were all alike."

"I hope he doesn't think that about me," Fannie told her, although conversations with him suggested he did. "I don't like being poor, but I don't mind working for what I want."

"Well, I wouldn't know what Mr. Clay thinks," the woman replied, her tone once again abrupt and unyielding. "As I said, it's bad manners to gossip. I'm here to teach you good table manners and nothing else."

"Thank you, Gerta," Fannie said, deciding she liked the woman despite her testiness. "I'll try not to disappoint you."

Clay arrived home early the following afternoon and found Fannie browsing through the family library. He leaned against the doorframe and watched her for a moment. The dress she wore was smart while remaining feminine and sexy. Close-fitting and cut above the knee, it showed off her figure and long legs. Her hair, pulled back from her face, cascaded down her back, almost to her waist.

"See anything interesting?" he asked after a minute, although he might have been asking himself the same question.

Fannie jumped at the sound of his voice. "Oh, I didn't hear you come in." She slipped a thick book on the history of Russia back in place, then glanced around the large room with its floor-to-ceiling bookshelves and oversize leather furniture. It was definitely a man's room, but with a vase of flowers, a couple of throw pillows, and a large afghan to cover her feet, she could imagine herself curled up on the large sofa in front of the fireplace with a book.

"Your father said I could look for something to read, but I don't think I'm going to find anything here to hold my interest."

"There's quite a selection."

"Yes, but not what I like to read."

"Which is?"

She blushed. "Love stories."

"Aha!" He walked inside, crossed the room, and motioned for her to follow him to another section of the library. "You just haven't been looking in the right place," he said. "See, my mother thought we should all be well-read, but she also believed reading should be for entertainment too. Here we are. Love stories, murder mysteries, spy novels."

"Oh boy!" Fannie checked the selection of

women's fiction and found a generous supply. She pulled one from the shelf and thumbed through it. "Thanks," she said, suddenly uncomfortably aware of how close he stood. She took a step back. "At least it'll give me something to do."

"Something to do?" He saw her blush, and he chuckled. "You're bored?"

"I feel as useless as a barrel with holes in it."

"I thought Gerta was going to spend time with you."

"She did. I can now spot the difference between a cocktail and salad fork at fifty paces. Hardly seems like an achievement worth writing home about, though, does it? Why are you grinning? Here I am miserable and you look happier than a pig in slop."

"I figured you'd get a kick out of playing lady of the manor."

"Not if this is all there is to it." She sighed and looked down at the linen chemise she wore with matching pumps. "I can't really do anything because I'm afraid I'll stain this dress. And if I walk too fast, these shoes'll fall right off my feet. Oh, Lord, I'm whining, aren't I?"

"What do you *want* to do?"

She shrugged. "I don't know. What do rich people do in their spare time?"

"It depends on what holds their interest. Some go boating or horseback riding. Others golf or play tennis. How about you? What do you like to do?"

She grinned. "Poor people don't have much spare time. And I haven't played much golf or tennis. The only thing I know how to do is bowl, but I'll bet you haven't spent a lot of time in a bowling alley."

"I've been in one or two in my life." He regarded her. He could sense her restlessness. "Look, if you want to go someplace, just say the word and I'll take you. You'll probably have to clear it with my father first."

The thought of getting out of the house for a while was a tempting one. "Oh, he won't mind. Besides, I need something to keep me busy so I'll stop thinking about what I'm going to say when my daughter steps off that plane tomorrow. I keep telling myself not to be nervous, but that's like trying to poke a cat out from under the porch with a rope."

He nodded as though it made complete sense. "We can get out for a while after dinner."

She was tempted to ask him to take her beforehand. Lord only knew what that fancy new chef was going to put on the table tonight. She'd already decided if it hadn't been raised on a regular farm, she wasn't eating it. "You think I could wear my old jeans?" she asked.

He chuckled softly. She had to be the first woman he'd ever met who didn't like nice clothes. Was it an act? He didn't think so. "You can wear any old thing you want. If it'll make you feel better, I'll wear my jeans as well."

"You're a nice guy, Clay. Nice guys are as scarce as a chicken leg after a church picnic."

The way she said it, sincerely and with conviction, startled him, and he remembered his promise not to let himself be drawn in by her and risk losing his perspective on the situation. "I'm not so nice," he said, shoving his hands into his pockets. "I thought I might need to move my things into your room tonight," he said. "I may not have time tomorrow. If you like, we can go ahead and get it over with."

Her stomach took a sharp dive. "N-now?"

"Your daughter is going to wonder what's going on if I'm sleeping in a room down the hall."

"She isn't coming until tomorrow. Couldn't we—?"

"We need time to get used to each other. Otherwise, the whole thing will seem stilted and phony."

It made sense, of course. It didn't matter that he knew her favorite flavor of ice cream or the name of the movie that always made her cry, they had to appear as though they'd been living together as man and wife for a time. "I suppose you're right," she said. "But I insist on helping you move your stuff. After all, you're doing it for me."

"That's fine. Let's go." He started for the

door. "By the way, have you talked to the old man about this?"

"This morning over breakfast."

"And?"

She thought it was nice of Clay to worry about whether or not something appeared improper to the rest of the household. Perhaps there was hope for father and son after all. "He understands completely. After all, there's nothing between us. We're only doing it for Mandy's sake."

"You told him that?"

"Of course. I wouldn't want him to get the wrong impression."

"Of course not," he muttered, and moved for the door once more.

Fannie followed him out of the library and up the staircase, where they found Gerta carrying a stack of towels. She did a double take when she saw Fannie follow Clay to his bedroom door.

"Fannie and I are moving my things into her room," he said as though it were an everyday occurrence.

"I see," was all the housekeeper said as a red-faced Fannie followed him inside.

His bedroom smelled of citrus and woods, a strange combination but a nice one nevertheless, Fannie thought. "What do you want me to do?" she asked, feeling shy in his room.

He handed her an expensive-looking travel case with his initials stitched into the leather.

"You can pack my toiletry items if you like." He motioned her in the direction of the bathroom.

She nodded and made her way across the room into a cream-colored tiled bathroom that had been wallpapered in a masculine-looking hunter-green. A picture of wild geese adorned one wall and a clay pot of dried flowers and cattails sat near the sink. The glass-enclosed shower drew her attention for a moment, and she found herself imagining Clay on the other side, naked and wet.

She shook herself mentally, knowing she had absolutely no business wondering about such things. She was not that sixteen-year-old who'd shared a biology class with him and wondered what it would be like to have him kiss her or walk her to her next class or ask her to the school dance. She'd learned a long time ago that being in a man's arms, while pleasant for the moment, did not make problems go away. If anything, it made them worse.

Finally, she opened the medicine cabinet, then hesitated once more before reaching inside for a bottle of after-shave. There was something decidedly intimate about going through a man's toiletries. She reached for the bottle, unscrewed the cap, and raised it to her nose. There was that smell again, making her stomach dip.

"Finding everything?"

Fannie jumped, almost dropping the bottle into the sink. She blushed and screwed the cap into place. She nodded quickly. "Y-yes. I was just . . . I like smelling this stuff."

He looked amused. "What do you think?"

She offered him a blank look. "About what?"

He chuckled. "About the way it smells."

"It's . . . uh . . . very nice."

"Yes, but you can't really tell by smelling it straight from the bottle." He stepped into the room, then leaned close. "Here, take a whiff. Tell me if you think I'm getting my money's worth."

Fannie raised her nose to where his jaw intersected with his throat, and her stomach fluttered wildly when the tip of her nose grazed the warm, hair-roughened skin. Once again, she caught a woodsy scent with just a hint of citrus, only this time she smelled male flesh as well. The combination made her head spin. She shivered, then stepped away, unable to make eye contact. "I'd say you're definitely getting your money's worth."

He continued to look amused. "Are you always this shy around men?" he asked.

"Of course not," she said defensively. "I have to deal with men every day."

"So it's me?"

She was thoroughly flustered. "I'm just not accustomed to standing in a man's bathroom going through his medicine cabinet."

"If this makes you uncomfortable, how are you going to share your bedroom with me over the next few days?"

"I thought you could sleep on the sofa."

"I could if I was six or eight inches shorter."

"Then, *I'll* sleep on the sofa, and you can have the bed."

"Ah, a liberated woman. Okay, I'll agree to that."

She glared at him, thinking how ungentlemanly he was for choosing the bed over the couch. Still, it was his house and he was doing her a favor by going along with her scheme, so she couldn't afford to make demands on him. "We'd best get back to packing," she told him. He slipped out of the room without another word.

The lovely cream-and-beige room that had appeared so large the first time Fannie saw it seemed to shrink in size the minute Clay stepped through the doorway. She couldn't help but wonder, not for the first time, how they'd manage over the next few days. Nevertheless, she decided it was probably a good idea for him to go ahead and move in so they could get accustomed to each other.

"Where should I hang my clothes?" Clay asked, pulling slacks, dress shirts, and sports coats from a hang-up bag. Since he'd only moved home the day before, he hadn't unpacked everything.

Fannie hurried to one of the closets and opened the tall ornate doors. "You can use this side," she said, shoving her own things out of the way. "The other closet still has your mother's clothes hanging in it."

He frowned as he carried his things to the closet and hung them on the rack. "My father needs to get rid of them," he said. "Or maybe he's keeping them out of guilt."

"I still have my mother's belongings," Fannie told him.

He glanced over his shoulder at her. "You think that's healthy?"

"I don't see why not. She might be dead, but she's still alive in my heart. I think about her every day. Sometimes, when I'm feeling lonely, I go to her grave and talk to her for hours. I can't tell you how much better I feel when I leave. Why, I wouldn't trade those times for a farm in Georgia."

He nodded, trying to decipher her words of wisdom, knowing it wasn't always easy. "Where should I put my folded clothes?" he asked, deciding his father's motives for holding on to his mother's belongings weren't so honorable. If he'd visited his mother's grave since the funeral, he wasn't aware of it.

Fannie pointed to a triple dresser. "I'm only using a couple of the drawers. Take all you need." She carried his toiletry items into the bathroom and put them in the oversize medicine cabinet next to hers. Once again, she was struck by an odd sense of intimacy.

Once Clay had unpacked, he stuffed his bags

in the back of another closet and closed the door. "Well, now, that didn't take too long," he said, dusting his hands. He walked over to the bed and sat down, bouncing several times to test the firmness of the mattress. "Which side of the bed do you sleep on?"

"I'm sleeping on the sofa, remember?"

"Yes, but I still need to know. In case it comes up."

"It won't." She was still irritated with him for not offering her the bed.

He smiled. "Humor me."

"I always sleep on the side closest to the bathroom. Satisfied?"

His smile broke into a grin. "You don't really have to sleep on the sofa. I was just giving you a hard time."

"I don't mind," she told him, "though I imagine it's a tremendous change for you, sleeping alone that is."

He looked amused. "Oh, well, it'll make me a stronger person in the end. By the way, I've been meaning to tell you, I like your hair that way. Worn down, I mean."

She was surprised how good the compliment made her feel, especially coming from him. "Thanks. You don't know how many times I've thought of cutting it off, but I can't bring myself to do it. My mother used to love to braid it, even when she got really sick. She asked me never to cut it."

"Sounds as if the two of you were close."

She nodded. "All we really had was each other." She paused. "I'm not sure it's worth being close to people, though. You always have to let them go in the end."

He wondered if she was referring to her mother or the men in her life, but he didn't ask. She had enough on her mind with her daughter coming, he didn't want to bring up sad memories. At the same time, he felt as if he could talk to her about almost anything. "Do you have a pair of sneakers with you?" he asked.

She nodded. "They're old."

"Doesn't matter. I was just wondering if you wanted to take a walk before dinner. Nothing strenuous. You can wear what you have on."

"I'd love to get out for a while," she told him. "Just give me a minute." She hurried to the closet and reached for her sneakers on a shelf. Clay stood by the window, looking out while she changed.

They exited the room together and almost bumped into Hyram, who was coming out of his own room. "All settled?" he asked, putting his arm around Fannie and squeezing her affectionately while his son looked on.

She nodded. "It'll be a bit cramped, but we should do okay. It's only for a few days."

"Did you ask Clay to bring out that folding bed from storage?"

Clay crossed his arms over his chest and wondered why he was questioning her about sleeping arrangements.

"It won't be necessary," Fannie said. "The sofa is plenty big enough for me. Besides, I don't want to have to worry about explaining a folding bed in case Mandy comes into my room." She glanced at Clay. "I mean *our* room."

"And you'll be going with Fannie to the airport tomorrow to pick up the girl?" Hyram asked his son. "Unless it's too much trouble," he added quickly. "I should have asked first."

"No trouble," Clay told him. "I assumed I would be taking her."

Fannie sensed the strain between the two men. "Clay and I were just about to take a walk. Would you like to come with us?" She secretly hoped he wouldn't so they could all relax. With his heart condition, he had no business getting worked up over anything. What she would give to be able to tell Clay as much.

Hyram shook his head. "No thanks. I've already had my exercise for the day. I just want to sit in my favorite chair and finish reading the evening paper."

"The *evening* paper?" she said, knowing Culpepper only had one daily newspaper.

Hyram chuckled. "If I have time to read it in the morning, I call it the morning paper. Otherwise—"

She grinned. "I gotcha," she said.

He winked at her. "You two have a good time."

Clay hesitated a moment, trying to decide if his father was being polite or if he truly didn't mind Fannie being alone with him. In a way, he resented the easy camaraderie between them and wondered why he'd never had that kind of relationship with his dad.

"Take good care of her," the older man told him. "I've gotten attached to her." He smiled and made his way down the stairs, leaving Clay with a hollow feeling in his gut.

FIVE

"You're awfully quiet," Fannie said, once she and Clay had walked a distance in complete silence. "Is something wrong?"

He looked baffled. "I'm just trying to figure out what's really going on around here."

"What do you mean?" she asked. "I thought we'd covered everything."

He stopped walking and regarded her. "I'm not referring to the business about your daughter. I want to know what's going on between you and my father."

"Your father?" she asked, clearly surprised. "I don't know what you mean." When he didn't answer, she went on. "This is all about money, isn't it?" she asked when nothing else came to mind. He didn't answer. "Why didn't you say something earlier? If you truly suspected I was after your father's money, you should have asked me."

"Would you have told me the truth?"

"I always tell the truth." She blushed. "Except for this one time with my daughter. And look at the mess it's gotten me in. As for your father, he and I are friends and nothing more."

Finally, he looked convinced. "*You* might feel that way, but I think he has something else in mind."

"Look, I didn't just fall off of some turnip truck. Your father has never given me any reason to believe his intentions were less than honorable. I think I'd know if he had something up his sleeve."

"He's handing over his home, isn't he? He hired extra staff to impress your daughter. I'd say that's a fairly strong indication of his affections."

"Are you always this paranoid?"

"When my old man does something nice for a pretty lady, I am."

Fannie took pleasure in the fact that he'd called her pretty, but she couldn't spend a lot of time thinking about it at the moment. She knew that Hyram Bodine's ulterior motives concerned his son and not her, but she wasn't about to get in the middle of that one.

She started to walk once more. Clay followed. "I wish you'd try to work out whatever problems you have with your father," she said. "He's very lonely, you know. And his health isn't what it used to be." She winced at her own words. Hyram would skin her alive if she revealed the business about the heart attack.

"I don't want to see him make a fool of you," he told her. "The way he did the others. I don't want him to use you."

"He's not going to *use* me. That's not the kind of relationship we have."

"You don't know—"

"I'm not a child, Clay. I'm perfectly capable of taking care of myself."

The look in his eyes was intense. "He'll start by giving you gifts. Small ones at first so you won't suspect. He'll ask your advice on everything, and you'll wonder how he ever made it without you."

"I don't want to hear any more of this."

He went on regardless. "Haven't you ever wondered why I stopped working for him and went out on my own in a completely different line of work?" He shook her slightly. "It's because I got sick of watching him treat women as if they were his personal property. I got tired of watching him cheat on my mother, of watching her pretend it didn't matter when he called and said he had to work late or go out of town for a few days."

Fannie could sense his rage. "You don't sound as though you like him very much."

"Maybe I don't." He paused, shoving his hands in his pockets, hunching his shoulders forward. He looked utterly miserable. "His first store was nothing more than a shack. He even sold fresh vegetables out of the trunk of his car at one time. My mother disgraced her family by marrying him, but her money turned the business into an empire." He shook his head sadly. "I've seen him wine and dine a lot of women with my mother's money."

"I hope you don't really think I'm after money," she said. "Or that I'd use your father to get what I want."

He remembered those short dresses, the rumors surrounding her in high school. They'd referred to her as the girl most likely, the one with round heels. He remembered the baby she'd given away. Now, here she was contradicting everything he'd ever heard or thought about her.

"You think I'm an opportunist?" she said when he remained thoughtful. "Is that it?"

"I don't want to believe it, but if you are, then I feel it's my job to protect my father."

She arched one brow. "Protect him?"

"From himself. He doesn't always use common sense where women are concerned." He paused. "I suppose that's not the only reason I'm hanging around. I have another, somewhat selfish motive."

"Which is?"

"You want the truth?" She nodded. "It sounds crazy, but I think it's because I want you for myself." There, he'd said it, admitted to her what he'd only allowed himself to believe.

She was dumbstruck, unsure she'd heard him right. "You're not making sense."

He surprised her further by slipping his arms around her waist and pulling her close. She blinked in surprise at the intimate contact their bodies made, but she didn't push away. "Life doesn't always have to make sense," he told her. "All I know is that I've been fascinated by you since I first laid eyes on you."

Her look was disbelieving. She remained still in his arms, confused and frightened and disoriented, like a small animal caught in the glare of headlights. "You certainly never gave any indication."

"You had your share of admirers."

This time she looked away. She didn't like to think of her high school years. She'd been naive, assuming boys liked her because she was a nice person. It wasn't until she'd heard a group of girls snickering about the way she dressed that she'd understood.

No wonder the boys flocked around her with the same enthusiasm children showed an ice-cream truck.

"I know why the boys liked me," she said. "I'm not a total nitwit."

"You didn't mind?"

"You don't know much about poverty, do you, Clay?" she asked sharply. "Maybe I had no choice as to what I wore. Maybe I had more on my mind in those days than how I looked." Such as how she was going to pay the bills, she thought, or how long her mother would remain in remission this time before the disease came back threefold. Somehow it seemed silly to worry about not having new clothes when there was medicine needed to make the woman more comfortable.

Clay gazed back at her, feeling dumber than dirt. He'd just assumed she'd liked dressing provocatively. Why was that? Why did he naturally assume the worst about people? When had he become so callous?

He sighed. "I'd like to get to know you better, Fannie," he said, wondering for the first time if he'd misjudged her, and cringing at the possibility. "I'd like to understand you."

He was much too close. She could clearly make out the dark blue, almost purple flecks in his irises, the stubble along his jaw. "Why?"

"Like I said, you fascinate me."

Her gaze was steadfast. "So does every woman under forty in this town. You really have no right to judge your father, you know. Your reputation isn't exactly lily-white."

"I'm not married the way my father was when he launched into his numerous affairs."

"The way I hear it, you run as fast as you can the minute a woman mentions marriage."

"So it makes me a little nervous. After seeing how miserable my parents were," he added.

"There are a lot of good, healthy marriages in this town. You shouldn't let your parents' unhappy union cloud your judgment."

He chuckled. "Look who's talking. I notice you haven't bought into the house and picket fence routine. Maybe you and I have more in common than we thought."

"Meaning?"

"Could be you're as gun-shy as me when it comes to matrimony. Wouldn't surprise me if it had something to do with the guy that ran out on you. Not to mention your father who split the minute things got tough."

"You sound as if you've got me all figured out," she said, her voice edged with sarcasm.

He smiled. His teeth were perfect. Someone had spent a lot of money on them. "Not quite," he said. "But maybe we can do something about it."

"Like what?"

"We could go away together for a few days. Once your daughter leaves, of course," he added.

His offer chilled her to the marrow. His wasn't the first such offer she'd received in her life. She was reminded once more of his closeness, the broad chest pressing against her breasts, the brush of his thighs against hers. She pushed away. This time she was successful.

"You're not the first man to invite me to share

a motel room, Clay. When a girl has a baby out of wedlock in this town, she has more suitors than she can shake a stick at. I'm not interested. We should get back. Your father will be worried."

"You misunderstood me," he said. "I was merely suggesting we get away from this place so we can concentrate on each other. I can afford double rooms."

"Sorry I misread your intentions," she said. "But the answer is still no."

"Why do you have such a chip on your shoulder?"

"I *don't* have a chip on my shoulder. But once my daughter goes back to Washington, I have to return to work. *If* I still have a job."

"I still say you've got a bad attitude toward men."

"And I'd say you don't handle rejection very well."

Once again, he reached for her. She tried to back away, but she wasn't fast enough. She was only vaguely aware of him ducking his head. The next thing she knew he was kissing her.

Fannie stood immobile, frozen by shock as he pulled her tight against him and covered her mouth with his. She parted her lips in surprise, and he sank his tongue inside where he began a thorough exploration. He tasted warm and masculine. Her heart took a perilous leap, her mind was thrown completely off balance. The kiss deepened.

She tried to resist, but it was only a half-hearted attempt, and they both knew it. He pulled her closer, flattening her body against his so she could acquaint herself with the sinewy feel of him. Her stomach fluttered, and she was filled with a strange inner excitement. His hands were big and warm at the small of her back. He dropped them to her hips and splayed them wide. She was startled by the intimacy.

He was the first to pull away. When he did, he found her staring back at him mutely, her lips red and swollen from his kiss. He smiled knowingly. "Not interested? You could have fooled me."

"I have to go," she said, her voice quavering.

"Coward."

"You're beginning to annoy me, you know that?"

He noted her fiery-eyed look and grinned. "That must mean I'm making progress."

She turned and started for the house.

"I'll walk back with you," he said, still grinning.

"It isn't necessary."

"Oh, but I insist. After all, my father distinctly asked me to look after you."

They made it back to the house in record time, walking swiftly, saying nothing. They found Hyram waiting in the study. "Oh, Fannie, I was just about to come looking for you," he said. "Come sit on the sofa beside me. I have a surprise."

Smiling and trying to hide her irritation with the younger Bodine, Fannie crossed the room and joined Hyram on the couch. She refused to look at Clay. "I love surprises," she said.

The older man returned the smile as he pulled a slender box from his jacket and handed it to her. "This is for you," he said.

She hesitated. Her smile faded slightly as a look of apprehension took its place. "What is it?"

"Why not open it and see for yourself?"

Fannie's hands trembled as she raised the velvet lid on the jewelry case. She found herself looking at an exquisite pearl choker with matching earrings. "Oh, my," she said.

"They belonged to my wife. She called them her lucky pearls. I want you to have them. Wear them when you go to the airport tomorrow to pick up your daughter. You'll be less nervous."

She was speechless. Stunned. She sat there for a moment, trying to think of something to say. What *could* she say? Thanks but no thanks? She could never accept such an extravagant gift. She raised her eyes to his and tried to think of a polite way of refusing the jewelry without hurting his feelings. His blue eyes were so sincere, they brought a lump to the back of her throat.

Fannie remembered suddenly they weren't alone. She glanced up and found Clay watching her, a knowing look on his face. She opened her mouth to say something, but he left the room before she could get the words out.

SIX

That same pearl choker felt heavy against her throat as Fannie climbed into Clay's car the following afternoon wearing a smart green linen coat dress and matching pumps. Wilhemena had come by during lunch to apply Fannie's makeup and put her thick hair in order.

"You look like a princess," the woman had told her as she ushered Fannie down the winding staircase to the main level. There was not the slightest hint of furniture polish in the air; yet, the banister and wood tables shined.

"I feel like one," she'd confessed. In just a few days, her life had changed dramatically from the uniform-clad woman who opened the Griddle and Grill at five A.M. each morning, worked till three, then studied until it was time to go to class. She no longer knocked around in jeans, sweat-shirts, and old sneakers; instead, she wore the very best Wilhemena had to offer. She felt like a storefront mannequin. It was all she could do to keep herself from getting mussed or stained or wrinkled. How she longed for her jeans.

Now, as Clay pulled out of the drive, Fannie wondered what he thought of her appearance. She didn't have to wait long for her answer.

"Nice necklace," he said, turning onto the main road.

She blushed. "I tried to give it back, but your father insisted I have it. Finally, I agreed to wear it today, just for luck. I would have told you as much if you hadn't stood me up last night. I thought we were going bowling."

He'd forgotten his promise to take her somewhere the night before. Instead, he'd gone back to his office and worked until midnight and thought of the land he so desperately wanted. And he'd thought of Fannie. "I'm sorry," he muttered. "I completely forgot. I guess I have a lot on my mind these days."

She suspected she knew what. "Why do you have to read more into my relationship with your father than there is? Can't you see he's simply trying to be nice? Don't you want him to have friends?"

Clay glanced at her. "Friends?" he said. "Do you have any idea what that choker is worth?"

She shook her head. "No, and I don't *want* to know." Her palms were already perspiring just thinking about it. She didn't feel safe carrying anything more than a twenty-dollar bill. She only hoped she didn't lose the dang jewelry before she could return it to Hyram.

He shrugged. There was a part of him that believed he was misreading his father's intentions and that the man had changed for reasons unknown to him. But each time he came close to fully believing it, the man said or did something to stir his suspicions. "He put you in my mother's room and now he's giving you her pearls. What's next?"

"Could we change the subject?" Fannie asked, pressing her fingers against her temples where she could feel the beginnings of a headache. "I'm already nervous about seeing my daughter."

His expression softened. "You're right," he said. "It seems I'm always sticking both feet in my mouth where you're concerned. Wish I knew why," he added, although he suspected he did. He was attracted to her, plain and simple.

"Let me know when you find out," she said dully.

They made the rest of the drive in silence, Fannie worrying about meeting her daughter for the first time, Clay reflecting on past relationships, what went wrong, how the experiences had changed him. Money made people greedy, he'd decided long ago, men *and* women. In school, he'd been the most popular boy in his class because of it.

First, when he was in the third grade, his mother had made him likable by installing brand-new playground equipment. When he was in middle school, she'd built a new library. Then there was high school, where he'd made captain of the football team after she'd offered to buy uniforms and remodel the gymnasium.

Later, he was pegged the most eligible bachelor in town. One date, and a girl was ready to spend the rest of her life with him. Funny how money brought out instant love and devotion in some people and made them love you regardless. Funny how it had managed to turn him into somewhat of a cynic. He hated being that way, but he was nevertheless.

The sign for the Savannah airport flashed before them, and Fannie moaned. "I'm scared, Clay," she said, her voice trembling so badly, it was hard to understand her.

He turned those compelling blue eyes on her. "You'll be fine." She had certainly made the transition from blue-collar worker to lady of the manor quite nicely.

She patted her hair. "Do I look okay?" She wasn't trying to draw compliments out of him, she was merely trying to work up the nerve to face her daughter.

He nodded. "You look every inch a lady," he said, knowing that's what she needed to hear at the moment. "And a very *pretty* lady," he added, unable to resist telling her as much.

She didn't feel pretty, but she appreciated him telling her so. She felt like a little girl playing dress up. "You're only saying that," she said. "But thanks, I needed to hear it."

He glanced her way. She looked so prim and proper sitting there, he couldn't help but wonder what she'd look like with her hair unpinned and mussed. "I never say anything unless I mean it," he said. "You should know that by now."

She wondered about the comment he'd made the day before, that he wanted her for himself. Her legs had turned to rubber at the time. Then he'd gone and ruined it by asking her to go away with him. Had she misunderstood? Did he truly have feelings for her or was he simply looking for a good time between the sheets? He could be so thoughtful at times that she suspected he genuinely cared. It was then that she allowed herself to care for him a little.

Fannie was still wondering about their relationship as they walked into the terminal a few minutes later. People were rushing back and forth with their luggage; busy executives sporting expensive briefcases, young mothers struggling with infants and toddlers and bulky diaper bags.

"We're early," Clay said, reading the monitor on incoming flights. "Would you like a cup of coffee?"

Fannie nodded, and they followed the signs to a restaurant and coffee shop. Once seated, her hands shook so badly, she couldn't hold her cup. She set it down.

"Hey, take it easy," Clay said, covering her hand with his. It felt small and delicate and brought out his protective instincts. "You're going to make yourself sick if you don't watch it."

"I can't help it. What if Mandy doesn't like me?"

"Why wouldn't she?"

She moved her hand, deciding it was easier dealing with frayed nerves than with the strange fluttering in her stomach that his simple touch evoked. If only he hadn't kissed her. If only he wouldn't show such concern.

"Because I gave her up," she said.

"You had no other choice at the time. I think it was one of the most unselfish acts you've ever committed," he added, then wondered when he'd changed his mind about her decision.

She looked torn. "I don't know," she said after a moment. "I've tried to convince myself I made the right decision. Even now I wonder how I would have taken care of her."

"There's your answer."

She shook her head sadly. "But she's my own flesh and blood, and I let strangers raise her." Her eyes teared. "Surely there was something I could have done. *Should* have done," she added.

Clay saw the tears and immediately felt flustered. The last thing he needed on his hands was a crying woman. He passed her his napkin. "This is not the time to cry, Fannie," he said, using the same tone a father might with his child. "You don't want to greet your daughter with red eyes."

She reached into her purse for a small mirror. "You're right," she said, blotting the corners of her eyes with the napkin. She blew her nose. "If I don't watch it, I'll have mascara dripping all over Wilhemena's dress."

He wasn't listening. He was noting how her tearful green eyes resembled emeralds. He wondered if another man had looked into those eyes and thought the same thing. He felt his gut tighten in response, and began to grind his back teeth together painfully. He pushed the thought aside, then realized he had experienced more feelings of jealousy the past few days than he had in his entire life, even during high school where it wouldn't have seemed so juvenile. What was wrong with him? Lord knew he didn't need to get involved with some woman, even one as desirable as Fannie. Especially now, now that it looked as though he was about to realize his career goals.

Problem was, he didn't want anyone else to have her either.

"You have beautiful eyes," he said at last, unable to resist telling her.

Fannie tried to mask her surprise, then covered her unease by checking her wristwatch. She wished he wouldn't say things like that to her. It only confused matters and made her think he truly meant it. She had to keep reminding herself it was only an act.

"I suppose we need to get to the gate," she replied as though she hadn't heard. She started to push her chair from the table. He caught her hand, forcing her to pause.

"You always seem to be running from me, Fannie," he said. "Why is that? What are you afraid of?"

She met his eyes. As always, she felt as if she could be swallowed up by them. She wondered what it would be like to look into those eyes while he was making love to her. A hot flush spread throughout her body. "What makes you think I'm afraid?"

"You back off every time things get the least bit serious between us."

"We have no business getting serious," she said, more to herself than him.

"Is there someone else?" he asked, then held his breath for her answer. He wished he'd thought to ask her in the beginning.

"No."

Relief flooded him. "Okay, if there's nobody else, then why are you afraid of letting me get close?"

She gazed back at him for a moment. "Until a few days ago, you didn't even know I was alive."

"My loss," he said. "But we didn't exactly travel in the same circles. Now that I've seen you again, I can't help but feel as if you've always been there, that our relationship should have progressed much further than it has at this point."

"Progressed further? You mean that we should be sleeping together?" she said, knowing where the conversation was leading.

"That's not what I meant," he insisted, although he no longer knew what he wanted or didn't want. "Sex plays a major role in any relationship. I would think it'd play a very satisfying role in ours." How many times had he imagined her naked in his arms recently?

She leaned closer. "We don't have a relationship, Clay. We're putting on an act, remember? This time next week I'll be back to flipping hotcakes at the Griddle and Grill and you'll be doing whatever it is you do. We'll pass each other on the street once in a while, but that'll be the extent of it."

"It doesn't have to be that way."

"For me it does. I've waited years to get my life on the right track, and I'm not going to let anyone or anything stand in my way."

"Stand in the way of what?"

"My education."

He looked confused. "What makes you think I'd stand in your way?"

"If we got involved, you'd start complaining about how busy I am, and I'd end up cutting back on my classes. That's the way it is for women. We're the nurturers of the world, always worried about those we love and putting ourselves last as a result." She thought of her mother who'd always put her husband first, working two jobs in order to support the family during the numerous times he was out of work. Where had it gotten her? In the end her husband abandoned her, and the job of caretaker had fallen to her daughter. As much as she'd loved her mother, Fannie had often wondered if she would ever be able to do the things she dreamed of.

Clay saw the look of determination on her face, and he wondered if she'd ever resented her sick parent. It was obvious she was impatient to get on with her life and education, and for some reason he wanted to see her do it. "What if I didn't ask you to give up your classes? What if I made it possible for you to give up the luncheonette instead?"

She arched one brow. "Are you offering to keep me?"

He didn't answer right away. "If I were, would you accept?"

She could see how curious he was and how much her answer mattered. She was tempted to tell him what he could do with his offer, but she didn't. Not because she had any intention of taking him up on it but because she knew perfectly well he expected her to jump at the chance. Hadn't he already made it plain what he thought of her by implying she was after his father's money?

"I'd have to think about it," she said, fixing him with a pleasant smile. "It'd be so tempting, committing myself to a man who had no intention of marrying me or giving me children, of having people refer to me as his mistress. What more could a woman ask for? I can't imagine why you haven't already found someone for the job."

"That's not at all what I meant," he said, growing impatient with her. "I was only hoping to help you."

"In exchange for what?"

"Oh, for Pete's sake!" he said. "Do you always have to suspect the worst? I'm beginning to think you don't have a very high opinion of men."

"Can you blame me?"

He sighed and raked one hand through his hair. "All I meant was, I could help you along with your finances. That way, you wouldn't have to work all the time, and we could see each other." He didn't like to think of not seeing her once they'd completed their mission. "As for the sex part—"

"It always comes back to that, doesn't it?"

"I wouldn't rush you. I'm not as eager to get you into bed as you think I am. We could let nature take its course, so to speak."

She was getting angry now. She leaned closer. "Let's get something straight, Clay. I don't *want* your stupid money. Nor your father's," she added, just so he wouldn't misunderstand. "If I *do* decide to go out with you when this is all over, which I doubt, it'll be because I want to, not because I feel obligated because you're paying my bills. And if we *should* end up in bed together, which isn't at *all* likely, it'll be because we genuinely care about each other, not because we're feeling lustful."

Feeling lustful? Surely there was more to it than that. Clay not only wanted to get her in bed, he wanted to hang around afterward and learn everything he could about her. Damn, why did they have all this other stuff to think about at the moment? Her daughter, his father, their completely different lifestyles.

"We really should go," she said, pushing away from the table once more.

This time he didn't stop her. He wanted to explore the possibilities of them getting together, but he needed time to think. He wasn't about to make promises he couldn't keep. Lord knew she'd had enough of that in her life.

"Allow me," he said, rising quickly. At her questioning glance, he went on. "Remember, I'm supposed to be the devoted husband. At least let me play my part with dignity."

She eyed him skeptically. "Just don't get carried away, okay?"

"Never." He stood behind her chair and waited until she rose to pull it out.

"Thank you."

"You're welcome. Shall we go?" He offered his arm.

Fannie hesitated, then took it. "The only reason I'm grabbing it is because my knees are shaking and I'm afraid I might fall on my face if I don't hold on to something."

He chuckled. "You're not fooling me. You're doing it because you like it."

She started to pull free, but he covered her hand and made it impossible. Together, they walked out of the restaurant and into the busy terminal, looking for all the world like the perfect couple.

"You're breathing hard," he said after a moment. "Something tells me it's not because you're excited over seeing your daughter." When she grunted, he shot her another disarming grin. "If you don't stop, you'll hyperventilate and pass out right here on the floor. Mandy will think you're drunk."

Fannie tried to calm her breathing. "I can't help it."

"Take a deep breath. That's it, slow and easy. Look, the plane is already here."

"Oh, Lord." Fannie waited anxiously for the next few minutes as passengers disembarked with painstaking slowness. She gripped Clay's hand so tightly, she feared it would be numb when she let go. Finally, a young girl stepped out of the crowd, carrying a shoulder bag.

"Clay, that's her!" Fannie said, motioning

toward the blonde who wore her long hair in a single braid down her back. "That's Mandy!"

"My God, she looks just like you!"

Fannie wasn't listening. She pushed through the crowd and made her way to the girl, who was looking like a lost chick. "Mandy!" The girl looked up when her name was called. She smiled, hesitantly, then made her way toward Fannie.

The next few minutes passed in a blur as Fannie embraced the girl tightly. She forgot her promise not to cry, tears streamed down her cheeks in small rivers. Finally, she took a step back and studied her daughter. "Oh my, you're beautiful," she said, her voice catching with emotion. "I would have recognized you anywhere."

Mandy laughed shyly. "You must be Fannie."

"Actually, it's Fannie Bodine," Clay said, coming up to stand beside them. "Hi, I'm Clay," he said, deciding Fannie would never remember to introduce him in her present state. "Fannie's husband," he added. He draped one arm across Fannie's shoulders protectively. "I can't tell you how much your mother has been looking forward to this moment."

Fannie was still crying. She noted her daughter's neat slacks and oxford shirt. "Oh, Clay, isn't she beautiful?"

Clay squeezed her shoulder. "Yes, she is, sweetheart. Just like her mother."

Mandy's gaze went from Fannie to Clay and

back to Fannie. It was obvious she was sizing them up. "Thank you for having me," she said.

"We're delighted you could come," she said.

"Yes, delighted," Clay echoed.

"And you're sure your parents didn't mind?" Fannie said. "I never got the chance to talk to them."

The girl hesitated. "They . . . uh . . . thought it'd be good for me," she replied.

"I'm glad to hear it," Fannie told her. "Really glad."

All three fell silent for a moment.

"I suppose we should get your luggage," Clay said, when it seemed neither of them knew what to say now that the introductions had been made and the small talk was out of the way. With him leading, they left the gate area and joined the throng of people moving through the wide hall. Clay saw how Fannie couldn't take her eyes off the girl. "Baggage is downstairs," he said, motioning to an escalator.

"Have you eaten?" Fannie asked her daughter as they stood next to each other on the down escalator. It was all she could do to keep from touching her constantly.

Mandy nodded. "They served a snack on the plane."

"My father has a special dinner planned for you," Clay told the girl when conversation lagged once more. "His new chef has been cooking all day."

Fannie smiled at his words, trying to look excited over the prospect of another dinner at the Bodine home. She only hoped they were serving something she recognized.

"Your mother tells me you're in eighth grade this year," Clay went on when Fannie continued to stare mutely at Mandy as though she feared she might dissolve in a puff of smoke at any moment. "How do you like it?"

Mandy shrugged, but the light flickered out of her eyes. "It's okay. I'd like it a lot better if there were boys. My . . . uh . . . parents decided to put me in a private girls' school this year."

They had reached the lower level. One by one, they stepped off the escalator. "Why'd they do that?" Fannie asked curiously, feeling it was important for her daughter to learn to interact with the opposite sex. Still, it wasn't her decision to make, she reminded herself.

"I suppose they think I'll get a better education," Mandy said, though her tone told Fannie she didn't share that belief. "Anyway, I'm trying to make the best of it. I'm assistant editor for the school paper. That's a lot of fun. Until we reach deadline and everybody starts snapping at one another. I'm also in the drama club. We just did *Romeo and Juliet*. I played Lady Montague. Everybody says I should audition for the lead role next time."

"That's wonderful!" Fannie told her, remembering how badly she'd wanted to join some of the clubs in high school. But between working and caring for her mother, she'd barely been able to manage passing grades. "And your grades are okay?" she asked, wondering if Mandy thought she was prying.

Mandy nodded. "I have to keep good grades in order to belong to the clubs. Also, I'm sort of expected to attend this college in Vermont when I graduate so I *have* to maintain a high average." She spotted the large conveyor belt containing various pieces of luggage. "Oh, there are my bags now." She hurried toward them.

"Sounds like an ambitious girl," Clay said when she was out of earshot.

"She's smart as a whip," Fannie said proudly. "You can tell by listening to her. She'll go far in this world."

Clay hurried forward once Mandy pulled a large suitcase and garment bag from the rotating baggage center. "Allow me," he said.

"They're heavy," she warned as though his fragile bones would crack under the weight. "We might need to rent a cart."

He merely grinned. He liked her already. She was a cute kid. "No need. I'm fairly big and strong for my age."

Mandy squealed in delight at the sight of Clay's car. "It's soooo cool!" she exclaimed as she waited for him to put her bags in the trunk. She climbed in the backseat and continued to look awed as he started the engine. "I'm used to riding around in boring cars," she confessed. "We own a Volvo station wagon. Can you believe it? And it's not red, it's gray. Gray seats, gray carpet, gray exterior." She rolled her eyes as she talked.

Fannie was awed, too, not by Clay's car but by her daughter's outgoing personality. She noted each facial expression, each little nuance. She tried to decide if there was a resemblance between the girl and her biological father. She saw none. There *was* a god.

The drive home took little more than an hour, during which time Mandy chatted nonstop and leaned between the seats frequently to adjust the radio. By the time Clay turned off the main road and followed the gravel driveway to the house, Fannie was looking forward to a little peace and quiet.

She noted Mandy's wide-eyed expression when they pulled up in front of the impressive mansion, and she was thankful she'd gone through with the charade. One only had to look at the girl to see she'd been raised by proper affluent people. She couldn't imagine taking her to the dumpy house she'd grown up in.

"How pretty," Mandy said, climbing out of the car and gazing at her surroundings through eyes the same green shade as Fannie's. She turned to her mother. "How long did you say you've lived here?"

Fannie smiled. "Not that long," she said, deciding to stick as close to the truth as she could.

"Your mother and I are sort of newlyweds," Clay said. "She's still getting used to the place."

"Oh, how romantic!" the girl exclaimed. "I had no idea."

"So if I have trouble finding the kitchen, you'll understand why," Fannie told her, laughing as if it were a big joke. She hoped the comment would pave the way in case she *did* actually get lost in the big house.

All at once, the front door was thrown open and Hyram appeared. "You're back!" he said, his eyes automatically coming to light on the thirteen-year-old. He smiled broadly. "You must be Mandy. Welcome to our home, young lady," he said.

The girl stuck her hand out. "Thank you for having me, Mr. Bodine."

"Just call me Hyram. Or Hy for short," he insisted. He cupped his hand under her elbow and prodded her forward. "You have to meet the rest of the gang."

Only then did Fanny realize they had company, Gussie and Ernestine Dempsey, and she decided Hyram must've been at work behind her back. She was touched. It was only right that her closest friends be allowed to share this very special occasion with her. She only hoped Hyram had schooled them in what to say should Mandy ask questions.

Gussie and Ernestine stepped forward, each wearing a shy smile, each dressed in evening clothes, or perhaps *over*dressed, Fannie thought, trying to smother a smile. Gussie, who was short and stout, wore a bright red dinner suit with a ruffled jacket that only made her seem wider. It was hard to tell how old the suit was, only that Gussie had added a few pounds since she'd last worn it. The gold buttons looked as though they'd pop off with her next breath. Ernestine didn't look much better in a burgundy-colored velvet dress that smelled as though it had spent a lot of years packed in mothballs.

"These lovely ladies are Ernestine and Gussie Dempsey," Hyram said. "You probably recognize the name. They're oil baronesses out of Texas." He didn't seem to notice the looks Fannie and Clay shot him.

Mandy shook their hands. "Pleased to meet you," she said politely. "I've never met a real oil baroness."

"You're the spit and image of your mother," Gussie said, then was nudged hard by Ernestine. She sputtered. "I mean, you bear a striking resemblance to her."

"Yes, striking indeed," Ernestine added.

"And this ravishing creature is Wilhemena Lightsey," Hyram went on, presenting the lovely platinum-haired woman. "She's into dress designing. Owns her own store and everything."

"It's indeed a pleasure," Wilhemena said loftily, holding out a perfectly manicured hand. She looked like something out of a magazine in an ivory silk cocktail dress. Mandy clasped her hand and shook it.

Gerta nudged Hyram.

"Oh, my, I almost forgot. This formidable-looking woman is my housekeeper," he said, motioning to the woman, standing tall and straight as a statue as she waited her turn to be introduced.

Gerta nodded respectfully. "It's an honor to meet you, miss. I hope your stay will be a pleasant one."

Hyram then introduced the chef and the maid, both of whom greeted Mandy with the same respect they would have royalty.

Clay leaned close to Fannie, his lips grazing her ear. "Don't you think your friends are overdoing it a bit?" he asked.

She shrugged. "They're trying to appear wealthy and influential. To impress Mandy."

Clay decided enough was enough. "I don't know about the rest of you, but I'm thirsty."

"Yes, let's go inside," Hyram said. "The new chef has prepared hors d'oeuvres, and I might as well tell you they look delicious."

The group congregated in the living room. Mandy took a seat next to Fannie. "You must enjoy living in such a pretty house," she said. "Would you take me on a tour later?"

"Of course I will," Fannie said, taking her

hand and squeezing it. She beckoned Clay with her eyes. "Maybe we can get Clay to go with us. He knows the history of the place."

"Be glad to," he told them as Gerta carried in a tray of melba rounds topped with liver pâté which had been glazed with aspic and looked quite festive. There was also caviar with toast points, accompanied by bowls of minced onion and chopped hard-cooked egg whites and sieved egg yolks.

Mandy shied away from the food, turning her attention to Wilhemena. "Did you design that dress you're wearing?" she asked.

Wilhemena smiled. "As a matter of fact, I did. Do you like it?"

"It's beautiful. I love clothes, but where I go to school everybody is forced to wear these dreadful pleated skirts that fall below our knees and make us look like somebody's old-maid aunt."

"That *is* dreadful," Wilhemena agreed. "I believe young ladies should be allowed to express their own individual tastes in clothes. It's all a part of growing up."

"I can't wait until I'm old enough to do as I please," Mandy said with vengeance, drawing a worried frown from Fannie.

Dinner was a show, put on for Mandy's benefit, and Fannie was touched deeply by the planning and hard work that had gone into it. As the chef flamed the chateaubriand tableside, she watched her daughter and wondered what she was thinking. Dessert was flamed as well; cherries jubilee over vanilla ice cream, served with demitasse.

"You guys really know how to eat here," Mandy said when it was all over and the young maid had cleared the table. "We don't go to this much trouble at home."

"Really?" Fannie asked, surprised by the revelation.

The girl hesitated. "Mom and Dad are very health conscious, you see. We'd all end up big as a house if we ate like this every night." She took in Fannie's appearance closely. "You must exercise like crazy to keep your figure."

"Your mother takes excellent care of herself," Clay said. "But one only has to look at her to know it."

Fannie glanced up at him quickly, blushing in response to the compliment. "Why, thank you, dear," she managed.

"Oh, I don't know why people are so worried about their waistlines these days," Gussie said. "I've always been on the plump side, but I'm as healthy as a horse."

"Which explains why you're forced to take blood pressure medication," Ernestine said.

"That has nothing to do with my weight, and you know it," Gussie told her. "If my blood pressure's a tad bit high, it's because those oil wells are driving me crazy." She looked at Mandy.

"There's a lot of pressure in being an oil baroness, you know."

"I'm sure there is," the girl said. "In which part of Texas do you live?"

"Which part?" Gussie said. She glanced at Ernestine.

"Uh, we live in the southern part," the other sister said. "Where all the oil is. But enough about us, Mandy dear. Tell us something of yourself."

"I'm afraid my life is rather boring compared to yours."

"You must know all the bigwigs in Washington," Wilhemena prodded.

Mandy shrugged. "I've met a few at charity functions, but I don't know many personally."

"Have you met Sam Donaldson?" Gussie asked wistfully. "I just love him and those sexy eyebrows."

"Afraid not," Mandy said regretfully. "But I could probably get his autograph for you."

"You don't know any good-looking senators, do you?" Wilhemena asked. "I wouldn't mind being married to a politician."

Mandy shook her head distastefully. "Most of them are old."

"Define old," Wilhemena said.

"Forty or so."

"Oh, jeez." The woman moaned, drawing laughter from the rest of them.

"Excuse me," Fannie said, wishing to spend a

few minutes alone with her daughter once Hyram suggested they move to the living room. "I'm sure Mandy would like to see her room now. Would ya'll excuse us? We won't be long." Both Hyram and Clay stood as the ladies made their way from the table.

Gerta passed them in the hallway. "I had Miss Mandy's things sent to the blue bedroom," she said, then pushed through a door that led into the kitchen, leaving Fannie standing there beside her daughter and wondering what to do next.

Where the heck was the blue bedroom?

SEVEN

"Is something wrong?" Mandy asked, gazing curiously at her mother.

"Huh?" Fannie chewed her bottom lip. Blue bedroom? Instead of saying anything, she led Mandy up the winding staircase. "Let me show you my room," she said, hoping to put off the inevitable.

"Your room?" Mandy said, arching one blond brow.

Fannie blushed. "Well, mine and Clay's, that is." She pushed through the door and stepped aside so Mandy could enter first.

"Wow!" The girl's eyes widened. "This is a radical-looking room."

Fannie chuckled and followed her in. "I assume that's a compliment."

Mandy walked over to the bed and slid her hand across the embroidered coverlet. "It's beautiful," she said, her voice a mere whisper. "It must be very old."

"I'm sure it is," Fannie told her. "This place is full of antiques. I'm afraid I don't know much about them."

"May I look around?"

Fannie shrugged. "Sure."

The girl checked out the bathroom and was even more impressed. She returned to the main room and took a seat on the settee facing the fireplace. "I'll bet it's cozy up here in the winter with a fire going," she said.

"Oh, yes," Fannie told her. "Very cozy." She took the chair opposite her. "This room belonged to Clay's mother before she died."

"What was she like?"

She hesitated. "I'm afraid I never knew her."

"His father is super."

"Yes, Hyram is very nice," Fannie said. "He's always made me feel welcome here."

"That's because he sees how much his son loves you," Mandy told her. When Fannie looked surprised, she went on. "It's obvious," the girl insisted, "just by the way he looks at you."

"Clay?" she asked, wrinkling her forehead.

The girl laughed. "Who else? Haven't you noticed how he watches every move you make? He's obviously head over heels in love with you."

Fannie was tempted to tell her Clay was probably watching to make sure she didn't steal the silverware while she was there. "I'm a lucky woman," she said instead.

"How did you meet?"

Fannie didn't have a problem answering the question, she and Clay had rehearsed that part. "In high school. I sat next to him in biology. I'm surprised I didn't flunk the course for all the attention I paid."

Mandy smiled. "I'll bet he was handsome even then."

"Oh, yes. Half the girls in school were in love with him."

"What attracted you most about him?"

Fannie paused. "I'd have to say it was his eyes. He's got the prettiest blue eyes I've ever seen." Her face took on a dreamy expression. "And his shoulders. They were so broad. I had such a crush on him."

"So you started going out?"

"Not right away," Fannie told her. "I would have had to stand in line."

"What do you think attracted him to you?" the girl asked.

Fannie paused, wondering what, if anything, Clay liked about her. She didn't have a clue. "I guess it would have to be my hair," she said at last.

Mandy nodded as though it made complete sense. "How did you know you were in love?"

Fannie wondered if all thirteen-year-olds were as inquisitive as her daughter. "That's simple," she said with more confidence than she felt. "I couldn't stand to be away from him. And every time he walked into a room, I just lit up. I felt . . . warm all over."

"I can't wait to meet someone and feel like that," Mandy said wistfully.

Fannie laughed. "Don't worry, you've got plenty of time. Just try to enjoy yourself and get your education first. It's not so easy to do those things with a husband and babies to care for."

Mandy was about to respond when a knock came at the door. Clay peeked in. "I just wanted to see if Mandy got settled in okay. Am I interrupting anything?"

Fannie shook her head. "No, please come in," she said, grateful he'd shown up. "Actually, Mandy and I were on our way to her room when we stopped off here. I'm supposed to take her to the *blue* room," she said, raising her eyebrows up and down like a Groucho Marx impersonator as she tried to make him aware that she didn't have the slightest idea where it was.

"We didn't make it that far," Mandy told him. "We've been chatting instead."

"Girl talk?" he said with a smile.

Mandy grinned. "Actually, we were talking about you."

"Me? Uh-oh. What'd I do?"

"Fannie was telling me what first attracted her to you."

Clay shot an amused look at the other woman. "And?"

"She says it was your eyes and shoulders."

"My shoulders?"

Mandy nodded. "She says you've got the widest shoulders in the world. Women like that on a man, you know."

Fannie could feel herself blushing. "Mandy, I don't think Clay's interested—"

"Sure I am," he said, coming over to sit next to Mandy on the sofa. There was a mischievous gleam in his eyes. "What else did she say?"

It was obvious Mandy thought she'd been caught up in a fun game between the two. "That she lights up inside whenever she sees you."

"No kidding?" He glanced at Fannie, saw two bright red spots on her cheeks, and grinned.

"I asked her what attracted you to her when you met, and she said it was her long hair."

His smile faded slightly as he took in the reddish-blond mass of curls that always made him wonder what it would be like having them brush his naked body as they made love. His gaze found hers. "Yes, your mother has beautiful hair. But that's not what first attracted me to her."

The girl looked surprised. "What was it then?"

He grinned and tweaked her nose. "I'm not about to tell."

Mandy looked vastly disappointed. "Oh, pleeease!"

"No way." He stood. "A man's entitled to a few secrets. Now, how about I show you to your room?" he suggested.

Fannie nodded quickly. "Yes, please do," she said. "Did I mention she's staying in the blue bedroom?" Once again she did the little dance with her eyebrows.

He looked amused. "Yes, I believe you did." He turned to Mandy. "That's just two doors down," he said. "Right across the hall from that big ficus tree. Come on, I'll show you."

Clay led Mandy out and showed her to her room, then returned a moment later where he found Fannie still sitting in the chair, staring at the empty fireplace. "You okay?"

She nodded. "She's all grown-up, Clay."

He stepped closer and put his hands on her shoulders. She stiffened at first, then relaxed as she grew accustomed to his touch. "Not quite, Fannie," he said as though unaware of what the physical contact was doing to her. "She still has a little ways to go." He paused and massaged her muscles. Fannie tilted her head back slightly and gave in to the sheer pleasure. "So, you like my shoulders, huh?"

Once again, Fannie blushed. "Mandy's full of questions about love. I suppose she's at that stage."

"You didn't answer my question."

"You have very nice shoulders."

He looked pleased. "You're wrong about the

hair," he said after a moment. "I mean, it's nice and all, but that's not what I find most attractive about you."

She was uncomfortable with the conversation. "I didn't know what to say. We hadn't rehearsed that part."

He nodded and made his way to the door. "Well, for future reference, let the record show that, even though I like your hair, I think you've got the prettiest, softest skin I've ever seen. I'm looking forward to seeing more of it." He kissed the nape of her neck, then left the room without another word.

"Fannie, please get in the bed," Clay said for the second night in a row as he stood over her in a pair of navy pajama bottoms that rode low on his hips and showed plenty of coarse black hair. "We've been through this several times. I was kidding when I said you had to sleep on the sofa."

Fannie pulled the blanket over her. "I'm fine," she said, wondering why he insisted on going without a shirt. She tried to keep her eyes from falling below his shoulders. If they'd looked broad before, that was nothing compared to how they looked now.

"I happen to know from past experience that thing is hard as a rock," he said. "Don't forget I grew up in this house. I can't tell you how many times I slipped into this room in the middle of a storm and tried to sleep on that settee. My mother usually felt sorry for me and told me to get into bed with her."

"It's really not that uncomfortable," Fannie insisted, although the previous night had proved just how far that was from the truth. The couch was narrow and about six inches too short for her. As a result, she was forced to lie on her side with knees bent. And it was hard as concrete, obviously designed more for show than comfort.

"Don't make me drag you to bed," Clay said, placing hands on hips. "You know I will. Besides, what's Mandy going to think when she comes barreling in here in the morning and finds us sleeping separately?"

"She'll knock first. I'll have time to get into bed."

"What if she forgets to knock?"

"Then, I'll lock the door."

He sighed heavily. She was stubborn as a three-legged mule. He blinked. Now, where had *that* come from? He'd obviously spent too much time listening to those little tidbits of wisdom she felt compelled to bestow on everyone who crossed her path. "Just get in the bed, dammit! You're making this difficult for both of us."

She raised up, bringing her sheet with her. "How am I making it difficult for you?"

"Because I can't relax knowing you're trying to sleep on that thing." He raked one hand through his hair, his patience worn thin. "Look, it's late and I'm tired. Either get in the damn bed, or I'm moving back to my room."

"You can't do that!"

"Wrong. I can do whatever I want."

In a huff, Fannie hauled herself from the sofa, grasping the sheet around her sarong style for modesty's sake as she made her way to the antique bed. It was high off the floor and not as wide as a modern-day full-size bed. She climbed up and wondered how they would share the space without bumping each other.

"Thank you," Clay said, making his way to the bed. He cut off the lamp and climbed up as well. He immediately rolled toward the center and sank into the feather mattress. He winced when his knee came into contact with something soft. He heard Fannie gasp. "Sorry," he muttered. "The mattress isn't very firm. It's stuffed with goose feathers. My mother claimed she couldn't sleep on anything else."

"That's okay," Fannie mumbled, scooting clear to the edge of the bed so they wouldn't touch. She lay there stiff as a plank, holding her breath, not daring to make the slightest sound. Even so, she began to sink toward the middle as well, where most of the weight was. Once again, she inched her way toward her side of the bed and grasped the mattress tightly to keep from sliding back. How she would ever sleep that way was beyond her. Worse, even though they were a good twelve inches apart she could feel the heat bouncing off his body like a pavement in summer.

Clay raised his head. "What the hell are you doing?" he asked, hearing her sounds of struggle.

"I'm trying to keep from sinking toward the middle," she said in frustration.

"God forbid," he mumbled. After a moment, he chuckled. "What's the matter, Fannie? Haven't you ever shared a bed with a man?"

She really wanted to belt him, but she didn't dare let go of her side of the mattress for fear of ending up in his lap. "I have a thirteen-year-old daughter," she said tightly. "What do *you* think?"

He didn't say anything for a moment. "Don't tell me that was the only time."

"I don't think it's any of your business."

"We're supposed to be married, remember? You should be able to tell your husband anything." He rolled over and propped himself up on one elbow. With the drapes open and moonlight spilling through the windows, he could clearly make out her profile. "Well?"

She could hear the amusement in his voice. "I never actually kept up with it," she said. "But tell you what. Once I know you better, I'll take you to my place and let you count the notches in my bedpost."

"Very funny." He followed the line of her hip beneath the sheet. He caught the scent of her perfume and wondered what it was. It was light but pleasant enough to make him want to move closer. "Were you ever in love?" he asked softly.

She wondered why he was so curious. Hadn't they already asked enough questions? She sighed. "I was once." She rolled over and saw that he was staring at her. She fixed her gaze on his face which was bathed in shadows. "I was very much in love with Mandy's father," she said. "Or as much in love as a sixteen-year-old girl can be. I thought he loved me too. At least he said he did. But he obviously wasn't ready to be a father."

"He's the only man you've ever . . . cared about?" he asked.

"Yes. I've gone out with a few, but nothing ever came of it. Until my mother died, I really didn't have much time on my hands. After her death, I went back to school so I was tied up with that and work. I really haven't missed not being involved with anyone."

He found it hard to believe. "Don't you miss being held?" he asked gently. "Or kissed?"

"You mean do I miss sex?" she asked. "The answer is no. In fact, I think the act is highly overrated. Not only did I find it uncomfortable, he left me the minute he found out about the baby."

"It usually hurts the first time," Clay said, unable to believe she'd only known one man. He reached over and grabbed a lock of hair and rubbed it between his fingers. "He was obviously young and inexperienced, Fannie. It doesn't have to be that way." He chuckled after a moment. "Hell, I remember my first time. We were in my mother's Lincoln Continental, sharing the backseat with about a million mosquitoes."

"Your point being?" she said, not wanting to skip down memory lane with him where his sexual escapades were concerned.

"My point is, it doesn't have to hurt. If a man spends enough time with a woman."

Something tugged her stomach. "Clay, I really don't think we ought to be having this discussion," she said.

His voice was like liquid velvet when he spoke. "We're both adults. It's obvious we're attracted to each other." He moved his hand from her hair to her bare arm. "What are you afraid of, Fannie?"

His touch sent tiny shivers up her arm. She snatched it away. The sudden movement made her lose her balance. She reached out, fumbling for an anchor of some kind, grabbed a pillow instead. The next thing she knew she was falling. Flailing arms took a lamp from the night table with her to the floor.

The thud seemed to shake the house. There was the sound of breaking glass. Clay raised up. "What the—?" He reached for the lamp on his side of the bed and turned it on. He leapt from the bed and ran around to the other side where Fannie, spread-eagle, was doing her best to sit up without cutting herself on a broken light bulb. "What happened?" he asked.

She snapped her head up, trying to decide if she was more embarrassed than angry. "I'd think it would be rather obvious," she said. "I fell off the damn bed."

"Are you okay?"

"Of course I'm okay," she said, blushing so badly, she was certain her ears glowed. "It's not as if I fell off the side of a mountain or anything."

He sighed heavily. He'd never known a more troublesome woman. "Be still," he said quickly when she started to move. "There's broken glass everywhere." He picked up the lamp and set it back on the night table, then knelt beside her and plucked several nasty-looking shards of broken light bulb from her. As he was doing so, he couldn't help but notice the nightgown she wore. It was elegant but fit her nicely, snug against her hips and breasts. He could see her nipples peaking through the thin material.

"Is that it?" Fannie said impatiently as his eyes combed her in a way that made her wonder if broken glass was the only thing he was looking for.

"You need to come out of that gown."

She arched one brow. "I beg your pardon?"

"It's probably covered with glass. Here, let me help you up." He reached for her hand and pulled her to her feet. "Stay here. You don't want to go anywhere and have glass fall in the carpet.

Tomorrow, I'll make sure this area is cleaned thoroughly. Now, where can I find something else for you to wear?"

"This is the only gown I have," she said.

"No problem." He hurried over to one of the triple dressers. He returned with the top to his pajamas. "Put this on."

"Here? Now?"

"I'll turn my back."

Fannie quickly pulled the gown over her head and tossed it nearby, then shrugged into his pajama shirt. The arms were much too long and the hem fell about midthigh. "Okay, I'm dressed," she said.

He turned around and grinned when he saw how big it was on her. "I didn't realize you were such a shrimp."

"I'm five seven and weigh one hundred and twenty-eight pounds. That hardly makes me a shrimp."

"Well, you've got short arms regardless." He reached for one sleeve and began rolling up the cuff.

"I knew I should have slept on the sofa," she muttered. "Do you think anyone heard me fall?"

His lips twitched with humor. "Only those within a five-mile radius."

"Then, why hasn't anyone knocked on the door to inquire?"

"Probably because they think we're having great sex, and they don't want to interrupt."

She snatched her arm away. He merely reached for the other. "This isn't going to work," she said.

"You're right. With that kind of attitude, nothing would." Ignoring her look, he finished with the second sleeve and released her. "Tell you what. We'll put a pillow between us. That way, you shouldn't have to come into contact with any part of my body. Now, can you climb up on the bed from where you're standing so you don't step on any glass?"

"I could if I was an acrobat," she said sharply.

"I could pick you up."

"No thank you." It seemed to her that he was making a big deal about nothing. Still, she had no desire to end up with a sliver of the broken bulb in her foot so, with a heavy sigh, she did as he suggested and managed to climb up on the bed from where she stood, giving him a good look at the new lace underwear Wilhemena had insisted she buy. While she arranged herself under the covers, Clay placed a bed pillow between them.

"Satisfied?" he asked.

She stared at the ceiling. "You're the one who suggested it."

"Only to keep you from falling out of bed again. Rather silly, isn't it?"

"Does this mean you want out?"

"I told you before, I won't back out on you. Now, can we go to sleep? I've already lost one night's sleep due to your ridiculous antics." He turned off the lamp and climbed into bed once more.

Fannie listened to him try to get settled. Ridiculous antics indeed! Did he have to make fun of everything she did? She lay there for a moment staring at the ceiling. It would have been easy to get mad at him, but she was tired of fussing. No matter what his opinion of her, and she had no way of knowing if it was good or bad at this point, he had gone out of his way to help her. They really should try to get along.

"This is the first time I've shared a bed with anybody since my mother died," she said after a while.

"Really?" He decided her mother must've been bad off to require that much attention.

"I'd sleep beside her those nights when she was sickest. Just in case she needed something or in case—" She paused.

Clay was suddenly curious. "In case what?"

Fannie didn't answer right away. "I was sound asleep the night it happened. I woke up shortly before daybreak, my heart pounding in my chest like a drum. I knew she was gone. She had died sometime during the night. Her body was already cool to the touch. I was thankful she went peacefully." She sighed. "Why am I telling you this?"

"Probably because you needed to talk about it," he said softly.

Fannie gazed at the ceiling, thinking of the

woman who'd played so many roles in her life; mother, best friend, and later, child. "Yes, I do miss her," she confessed. "She was really the only friend I'd ever known."

"How come?"

Fannie hesitated. Even now it was painful to talk about the past. "Most of the girls at school looked down on me," she said. "My family was white trash. They accused me of dressing like a tramp because my skirts were so short and tight. I was too proud to tell them I couldn't afford anything else."

Clay frowned in the dark. "What about the boys?" he asked, although he suspected he knew more about it than she did. He remembered how they talked about her in the boys' locker room. "How did they treat you?"

Fannie turned her head so that she was facing him. "You should know the answer to that one, Clay. Anytime I went out with a boy, he would try his darnedest to get to home base. It didn't matter that he didn't succeed. Come Monday morning he'd have it all over school how he'd scored with Fannie Brisbane. After a while, I just stopped accepting dates. By that time my mother was too sick for me to leave her much. It didn't matter." She was lying. It had mattered.

He was quiet for a moment, dealing with feelings of foolishness and sudden anger. The world could be so cruel at times. "I'm sorry you had to go through that," he said at last. "Especially with what you were dealing with at home." He paused once more, hating to have to admit his part in it but feeling the need to confess. "I suppose I was no better than the guys who made up the stories. I mean, I listened to them. And believed them," he added on a quieter note.

"How come you never asked me out?"

He shrugged in the dark. "I guess I figured your date card was full. I'm sorry I thought the worst of you, Fannie. I'm usually pretty good about figuring people out."

"You were young," she said. "We both were. Anyway, I guess I deserved what I got. I ended up going to bed with the first guy who was good to me. The first one who didn't treat me like a slut. I thought he was different. Boy, did I get the surprise of my life."

"But look what became of it. You have a beautiful daughter."

She sighed softly. "Yes. Just seeing her and knowing how well she's doing makes it worthwhile. I'd go through all that pain and uncertainty again."

"Good night, Fannie."

She told him good night and closed her eyes, feeling less anxious about sharing a bed with him.

EIGHT

"Where the hell could she be?" Clay asked, standing in the door of the dining room where the young maid was serving breakfast.

Fannie shook her head. "I've no idea. I looked in her room, and she's gone."

Gerta caught the tail end of the conversation as she came into the room. "Are you asking about Miss Mandy?" she said. When they both nodded, she went on. "The child got up with the chickens this morning. Said she was too excited to sleep and wanted to go for a walk. I told her there were bicycles in the garage if she wanted to use one."

"Did you see which way she went?" Clay asked.

"She was headed toward the Elderberry place."

"Oh, damn!" Clay muttered.

The older woman looked frightened. "Is something wrong?"

"What if she talks to somebody?" Fannie said frantically. "You know what a gossip Maud Elderberry is. What if she finds out—" She paused. "You know."

"Oh, my," Gerta said. "I hadn't thought of that."

"Let's go," Clay said, grabbing Fannie's hand and pulling her toward the hall and front door. Hyram, coming down the stairs in his bathrobe, called out.

"Where's the fire?" he asked.

"Mandy's out riding one of the bicycles this morning. We have to find her before she has a chance to talk to anyone." They were out the door before the older man could question them further.

Once they were fastened inside Clay's car, he started the engine and peeled out of the circular drive, then drove the quarter-mile distance to the main road. "I knew this wasn't going to work," he said, his eyes combing the area for a young girl on a bicycle.

"So did I," Fannie muttered. "I mean, I wanted to believe it would because it was so important to me, but this is what happens when you lie and lie and lie about something. Sooner or later, it catches up with you."

"What are you going to do?" he asked.

"What I should have done all along. Tell her the truth."

"Well, she seems like a nice kid. I don't think it's going to change her feelings about you one way or the other."

Fannie was searching frantically for some sign of her daughter. "I don't know, Clay," she said wearily. "She might look down on me. I've spent my whole life trying to prove to the people in this town that I'm not white trash. It would kill me if—"

"Mandy is *not* going to think that about you," he said angrily. "You're the one with the hang-up about what people will think."

"What are you talking about?" she said testily.

"You're the one who feels you have to prove yourself just because of what your father did."

"He couldn't keep a job. He wrote bad checks all over town. He abandoned his family."

"But that was *him*, not you. You could no more control that than you could the weather. But you refuse to let it go. Otherwise, you wouldn't have been compelled to put this elaborate scheme together for your daughter in the first place. When are you going to realize you're good enough just the way you are?"

Fannie was only half listening, so intent on finding her daughter, nothing else mattered. She finally spied her standing beside a corral of horses on the Elderberry property. "There she is!" she cried.

Clay braked and turned sharply to the right, spitting gravel as he did so. Mandy, who was talking to the Elderberry's oldest son, looked startled at first but smiled the moment she recognized them. She hurried over.

"Dwight was just showing me his horses," she said. "Aren't they beautiful?"

Fannie got out of the car, searching her daughter's face for some sign that she knew the truth. She saw nothing. "Yes, they are beautiful," she said. "We were worried about you, Mandy."

"Worried about me? Why? I told the housekeeper where I was going. This town feels pretty safe to me."

Fannie knew the girl would think she was overreacting to her taking a simple bike ride, but she couldn't very well tell her the real reason she was anxious. Fortunately, it seemed the only thing Mandy and Dwight had discussed was horses. Fannie smiled as she pulled a strand of blond hair from her daughter's face. "I guess I'm just being overprotective this morning," she confessed. "Are you hungry? There's a big breakfast waiting back at the house."

"I'm starved," Mandy told her. "Let me say good-bye to Dwight and grab the bike."

Fannie climbed back into the car and sighed her immense relief. "I don't think she knows anything."

Clay looked relieved as well. "Good. We'll just have to watch her more carefully. Tell you what, we'll keep her busy at home today, then tomorrow we'll get up early and drive to Savannah and spend the night. We have to be there early Monday morning anyway, so she can catch her flight back."

Fannie felt her stomach lurch at the thought of her daughter going back home, but she knew that's the way it had to be. She would simply have to treasure each moment they had together. "That sounds like a wonderful idea," she said. "If you're sure you can spare the time away from work."

"I wouldn't have offered otherwise."

"Okay, I'm ready to go," Mandy said, coming up beside the car on her bicycle.

The Elderberry place was only a mile from the Bodine mansion. Mandy rode her bicycle in front of the car, and Clay followed slowly and at a safe distance. Once they pulled in and started for the house, Mandy began telling them about the beautiful mare that Dwight Elderberry said she could ride whenever she liked.

"Do you ride?" Clay asked.

The girl nodded enthusiastically. "My best friend's parents have a farm in Maryland. I go up there with them once a month, and we ride until our tailbones are sore."

They were on the front porch of the house. Clay opened the door and held it for the ladies.

"You know we have horses here," he said matter-of-factly. When Mandy looked surprised, he went on. "There's a stable out back. You can't see it from the house because of the trees. I'll take you riding after breakfast if you like."

Mandy nodded excitedly. "That'd be super. Do you ride?"

"I haven't in a long time. But I imagine I can still sit on a horse without falling off."

Hyram was halfway through his breakfast when they came into the dining room. Mandy told him about meeting cute Dwight Elderberry and Clay's plans to take her riding. Hyram turned to Fannie.

"Are you going with them?" he asked.

She shook her head. "I'm afraid I don't know the first thing about horses. Actually, I'm a little bit afraid of them."

He reached over and patted her hand. "You can stay here with me," he said. "I'm having a truckload of flowers and shrubs brought in this morning. Perhaps you can help me decide where to place them."

"Of course, I'll help," she told the older man with a smile, remembering how much pleasure she'd derived from her vegetable gardens over the years. Her smile faltered as she glanced across the table and found Clay watching her, a frown marring his handsome face.

❧━━━━━━━❧

The stable smelled of fresh hay and manure. Clay chatted briefly with the elf-sized man they employed to take care of the horses, chuckling as Mandy enthusiastically greeted a large liver-colored quarter horse named Sam and a spotted mare named Bitty.

"Come with me and I'll show you my dad's pride and joy," Clay told her, leading her to the end of the stable. A gray Arabian stuck his head through the opening and snorted loudly.

"Wow! He's beautiful," she said. She slowly raised a hand to rub his forehead.

Clay nodded in agreement, taking pride in the animal as well. His head was small with protruding eyes and wide nostrils, markedly different from the American breeds they owned. "This is Nadja," he said. "My father bought him from a famous stud farm in Saudi Arabia."

"What's he going to do with him?"

Clay shrugged. "He was going to stud him out. Then he decided he'd raise them, but this is as far as he got."

"What happened? What changed his mind?"

Clay shrugged as though he didn't have a clue, but he suspected it was because he'd thrown out the person who'd instigated the whole thing. How long was he going to hold a grudge over that, he wondered, feeling ridiculous now for resenting what time Fannie spent with his father. She'd made it plain that she and Hyram were nothing more than friends, and his gut told him she was being truthful. So why was he still acting like a jerk?

"If you want to ride, I suggest we have the stable man saddle Sam and Bitty," Clay said after a moment. "This one has been known to be skittish at times."

"I'd love to work with him," Mandy said. "My friend's father taught me how to handle horses."

"Maybe you can," he said. "There's always the summer. You're welcome to visit anytime." Clay wanted to kick himself the minute he said it. This was all a charade, a hoax put on for Mandy's benefit. Come Monday afternoon, when she was on a plane headed back to Washington and ultimately another part of the world, the whole thing would fold up and be no more.

"That's going to be rather difficult, isn't it?" she asked.

"What do you mean?"

She didn't quite meet his gaze as she answered. "Dwight Elderberry and I didn't confine our conversation to horses."

Oh, hell. He studied her. Her expression gave nothing away. Maybe he was jumping to conclusions. "Oh yeah? So what else did you talk about?"

"It's all over town, Clay, what you and my mother are doing. You aren't really married. And she isn't what she's pretending to be."

He didn't know what to say at first. Finally,

he decided all he could do was try to explain. "I'm sorry, Mandy. We didn't do it to hurt you. Your mother didn't want you to be ashamed of her. She was afraid if you saw how she really lived, you might not want to visit her again."

The girl seemed to ponder it. "Actually, I feel better knowing she's not rich." When he looked confused, she went on. "I was told from the beginning that my real mother loved me very much, but that she was forced to give me up because she was poor and had an invalid mother to care for."

"That's, in fact, the way it was."

Finally, she looked at him. "So how do you think I felt when she wrote telling me how she was happily married and living in this fine house with servants. I couldn't help but wonder if maybe somebody had lied to me, that my mother was really a wealthy socialite who didn't want to be bothered with a brat."

He shook his head emphatically. "That's not the way it was at all, Mandy. Your mother has had a hard life. Harder than anyone I know. But she's too proud to admit it, even to those closest to her. Not only that, I think she panicked when you told her your father was a big shot with the State Department. She figured you were used to better than what she could offer."

Mandy's eyes clouded for a moment. "Would you tell me the truth about her?"

He sat on a bale of hay and motioned for her

to join him. "Your mother's a very special person," he said once she'd taken a seat beside him. He told her about her father abandoning the family and how Fannie cared for her mother until she died years later. "The house she lives in isn't much to look at," he said, "but it's paid for and allows her to make payments on her mother's doctor and hospital bills. She works at the luncheonette in town and goes to school at night."

"And she thought I would be ashamed of her for that?" Mandy asked disbelievingly.

"I'm afraid so." He smiled and tweaked her nose. "I think it's time the three of us sat down and had a good talk. Fannie should have told you the truth from the beginning."

"I don't want you to tell her I know," Mandy said. "I want her to tell me herself. When she's ready," the girl added.

"It's gotten out of hand," Clay said.

Mandy shook her head. "No, Clay. Please don't say anything yet."

"Don't say anything about what?" a feminine voice said, causing them both to jump.

They jerked their gazes toward the stable door. "Oh, hi," Mandy said.

Fannie reached over and tucked a strand of hair behind her daughter's ear. "What don't you want Clay to say anything about?"

"Huh?" Mandy glanced at Clay, her eyes pleading for understanding.

He felt sorry for the kid. "Uh, Mandy isn't as knowledgeable about horses as she led us to believe," he said, unable to think of anything else.

"Oh?" Fannie gazed at her daughter curiously.

Mandy sighed heavily. "Yeah, I wanted you guys to think I was really good with them, but I guess I'm not. I sometimes do that, you see, make people think I'm better at something than I really am. Like playing Lady Montague. I wasn't really all that good doing that either."

Fannie was genuinely confused. "But why would you be ashamed to admit something like that?" she asked. "People are good at some things and not so good at others."

"I can't think of anything that I'm particularly good at," the girl replied. "My aunt Rhea says I'd better find a wealthy husband to take care of me because I can't seem to do anything right."

Fannie bristled at the thought of anyone saying such a thing to Mandy. "Your aunt Rhea?"

"She's my mother's half-sister. Seventy years old, need I say more? She thinks today's youth are lazy and good for nothing. I think she longs for the old days, before child labor laws came into practice. Nothing builds a kid's character like a good sixteen to eighteen hours in a sweat factory."

Fannie was at first horrified, then decided Mandy had to be exaggerating. She glanced at Clay and wondered what he made of the remark.

She couldn't tell. "You're not serious," she told the girl.

"As serious as a heart attack," Mandy replied.

"Well, I hope your mother doesn't feel that way about children," Fannie said, knowing she had no right to offer her opinion but unable to resist doing so anyway.

Mandy's expression softened. "Naw, she's nothing like her sister."

"Good." Fannie clasped her hands together in front of her. "I'm sure Clay can show you all you need to know about horses," she added gently, then looked to him for confirmation. "Can't you?"

"I'll be glad to."

She smiled at her daughter. "Stop worrying so much, it'll be okay." She chatted for a moment more but saw that Mandy was anxious to get started on her lesson. She turned for the door, then paused. "Oh, the reason I came out. I was thinking of preparing us a picnic lunch for later . . . after your riding lesson. We can eat on the patio if you like."

"That sounds good to me," Clay said, wishing the two women didn't have so many secrets between them.

Mandy nodded. "Yeah, sure. That sounds great."

"How do you think it went today?" Fannie asked Clay once he'd climbed into bed beside her, maintaining a respectful distance so she wouldn't feel compelled to throw herself over the edge the way she had the night before.

"All right, I guess." He was still thinking about his conversation with Mandy in the barn, and his promise to keep it secret.

"Just all right?" she asked, arching one brow. Mandy had thoroughly enjoyed her ride with Clay, faring much better on a horse than Fannie would have thought possible after the girl had made such a big deal out of not being very good. Fannie suspected the girl didn't have a whole lot of confidence. What bothered her more was the fact that a family member might be contributing to those feelings of insecurity. It sounded to Fannie as though Aunt Rhea could use a good throttling.

Nevertheless, the picnic had been a huge success. Fannie had temporarily moved into the kitchen and fried enough chicken for a church social while the chef prepared a delicious potato salad vinaigrette, an assortment of cheeses to go along with a loaf of crusty French bread, and leftover sticky pecan buns for dessert. They'd washed it down with mint-flavored iced tea and had listened as Clay told funny stories about growing up.

"I have a question," Clay said, drawing her back to the present. "What would you do if you'd promised someone not to tell something, but you think it's in their best interest to go ahead and get things out in the open?" He wasn't usually so indecisive, but the two females in his life were making things awfully confusing.

Fannie bolted upright from the bed, certain he was about to blow her cover. "You shouldn't tell, Clay, no matter what. You may not always understand why people do the things they do, but if someone has trusted you enough to keep something secret—" She paused. "It's not your place to tell," she added.

He pondered her words as he gazed at her, hair falling down her shoulders in a mass of waves and curls. He wondered if a woman had ever looked more desirable in a man's pajama shirt. He wondered if she had any inkling of how much he wanted to kiss her. "Don't go getting your pistol all fired up," he said, then sighed at his choice of words. "I was just curious."

"So you won't say anything?"

He found himself mesmerized by her lips and the little indentation at the top that formed their bow shape. Her nose was perfect, slightly tilted at the end with a smattering of youthful freckles. And her eyes. So green. They sparkled like something in a jewelry store display case. He sighed and wondered how they could have lived in the same town without getting to know each other better. He wondered if he should take a chance on getting to know her now, wondered how he would ever let her go when all this was over.

"You didn't answer the question," Fannie said, wishing she knew what he was thinking. The bed covers were pulled to his waist, exposing that powerful chest, feathered with crisp black curls. She couldn't keep her eyes off him. It was all she could do to keep from raking her fingers through those curls. She couldn't remember the last time she'd been attracted to a man, but she'd been attracted to Clay Bodine from the very beginning.

"Why don't you?" he said, as though reading her mind. "It won't kill you to touch me."

Fannie snapped her head up, and their gazes collided. "What—?"

He chuckled, reached forward, and grasped her under the arms, pulling her flat against him. She gave a small yelp of surprise, then squelched it, realizing there were other people in the house. "Stop fighting me," he said, noting the anxious look in her eyes. "It's time we both stopped acting like idiots . . . time we gave in to this crazy thing between us."

She resisted but only halfheartedly. She wished he hadn't taken a shower before bed, he smelled so good, so fresh and clean and male. "I don't know what you're talking about."

"You want me to kiss you as badly as I want to. And you know what? I'm going to do just that." He no sooner got the words out than he cupped a palm at the back of her head and pulled her close, then captured her lips with his. She tried to pull free, then wondered why. Why was she trying to escape the delicious taste of his mouth? Wasn't that what she'd always secretly wanted? He slipped his tongue past her lips, and all coherent thought ceased. She found herself kissing him back, snaking her arms around his neck and giving in to the sheer pleasure of his embrace.

As the kiss deepened, something stirred low in her belly, pleasant and warm but making her all at once anxious. She pressed one hand flat against his chest and delighted in the springy texture of his hair. As she slid her fingers through, the curls coiled around them. She could feel him becoming aroused.

Her first thought was to retreat. Hadn't she been hurt badly before? Yes, but she was a woman now, not some naive teenager who believed everything a man said. Besides, she could no more pull away from him than she could will her heart to stop beating. She had spent too many years wondering what it would be like in his arms. Ever since biology class she had wondered, every time she had passed him in the hall or spied him on the street with his friends. Years later, when she'd driven by a building site and happened to see him standing among the clutter, she'd wondered again.

Clay broke the kiss, and they both sucked in

air. "I've never wanted a woman so badly in my life," he said, his voice slightly hoarse.

She felt the same way. Despite her reservations, despite the chance she would be taking by caring for him. But didn't she *already* care for him?

"Clay—" Her mouth was as dry as a desert wind. She swallowed and tried again. "As much as I'd like to, I just . . . can't."

"Can't or won't?" He groped for her meaning.

"I could get pregnant."

"I could maybe pick up something."

"Now? It's eleven o'clock. The drugstores are closed." Actually, she was glad he wasn't prepared for a roll in the hay.

"I filled up with gas today at the station in town. They had one of those dispensers in the men's room."

She frowned. "Dispenser?"

"A condom dispenser."

"Oh." She blushed.

"I could be there and back in less than twenty minutes."

She thought about it. "I'll go with you," she said, knowing she'd change her mind if she waited alone. How unromantic to have to worry about such a thing. Still, it was necessary. She pushed away from him, and he released her. "Let me grab my jeans."

They were ready in a matter of minutes,

sneaking through the hall, down the staircase, and out the front door. A full moon guided them to Clay's car. He helped her in, then joined her in the front and started the engine.

"Jeez!" she whispered. "Do you have to be so loud?"

"It only *sounds* loud," he told her. "It's not really."

She looked at him, frowning, trying to make sense of what he'd said.

They made the drive in record time, pulling into the gas station beside the pumps. Eustace McIntyre hurried out of the station in moss-green overalls.

"Clay, m'boy," he called out, tucking his head into the window. "What are you doing back? I sold you a full tank today."

Clay looked at Fannie, then back at the man. "Uh, we were taking a drive and the oil light came on," he lied. "Thought I might get you to check it."

"The oil light, huh? What d'you know, I could'a swore I checked it today." The man went around front. "Well, let's open her up and have a look-see." He waited for Clay to pull the hood release, then lifted it.

"Okay, go," Fannie said. "Now's your chance." She nudged Clay, wanting him to hurry up so they could get out of there.

He climbed out of the car. "Mind if I use the men's room, Eustace?" he asked the owner.

The older man looked up as he pulled the oil stick from beneath the hood. "Can't do that, son."

Clay almost tripped over his own feet. "Beg your pardon?"

"Out of order. You'll have to use the women's bathroom."

Clay sighed and rolled his eyes. Fannie shook her head and looked the other way. It was just as well, she thought. She wasn't ready for any kind of relationship.

"Come on, now, Eustace," Clay said. "All I need to do is wash my hands. I'd feel like a sissy going into the ladies' bathroom."

Eustace nodded as he slid the oil stick back into place and puttered beneath the hood. "Okay. You know where to find the key. Just don't go flushing the toilet or you'll find yourself ankle-deep in water."

A moment later, Clay appeared at Fannie's window. "You got any quarters? All I have is bills."

Fannie remembered the roll in her purse, reached inside, and handed it to him. "Just take them," she said when Clay arched both brows at the ten-dollar stack.

"You really don't think we're going to need this many?"

She blushed. "Of course not."

He grinned. "Good. I'm not eighteen anymore, you know."

"Would you just go!"

Eustace was closing the hood when Clay came out of the men's room a few minutes later. "There ain't a dang thing wrong with your oil," he said. "Are you sure it was the oil light that came on?"

Clay snapped his fingers as though he'd remembered something important. "You're right," he said. "You put half a quart in today."

The man rubbed his chin as though truly baffled. "Could be a fuse goin' out, though it doesn't seem likely. Once you blow one of those puppies, they just go out and don't come back on. I could put in a new one, just in case. Take me five minutes is all."

"No time, Eustace," Clay said. "I've got a sleepy passenger on my hands." He motioned to Fannie. "Got to get her home before she conks out in my front seat."

"I thought that was you, Miss Brisbane," Eustace said, peering inside the car and tipping his cap. "You're out mighty late, ain't you, seein' how's you got to open the Griddle and Grill so early."

"I'm taking her home right now," Clay said, opening his door and climbing into the seat beside her.

"Don't forget to drop by so I can have a look at that fuse." Eustace was still watching them curiously as Clay pulled out of the drive onto the main road.

Hyram was coming out of the kitchen with a cookie and a glass of milk when Clay and Fannie let themselves in the front door. "What's going on?" the older man said, glancing from one to the other.

"Neither of us could sleep," Clay whispered, hoping nobody else was going to get up. "We took a drive."

A sound on the stairs made them look up. Mandy was standing at the top rubbing her eyes. "I thought I heard a noise." She joined them in the foyer. "Oh, milk and cookies," she said, licking her lips. "May I have some?"

"Sure you can," Hyram said. He glanced at Clay and Fannie. "Ya'll want something? You really should join us, you know, seeing as how you woke us."

"Uh, sure," Fannie told him, noting the look Clay shot her.

"Hey, does anyone play cards?" Mandy said. "That's a good way to pass the time when you can't sleep."

"I know right where Gerta keeps a deck," Hyram replied. "Come on."

Fannie shot a look of apology toward Clay and followed.

They played until three, using toothpicks instead of money. Finally, Fannie gave up when she couldn't stop yawning and the faces of the cards blurred before her. Clay folded as well and followed her up the stairs to their bedroom, where she immediately locked herself in the bathroom to change. She came out a moment later wearing his pajama shirt and literally staggered toward the bed. She was asleep the minute her head hit the pillow, only half covered, one slender leg taunting him.

Clay sighed. "So much for romance," he mumbled. "Guess that leaves me with nothing to do except take a cold shower."

NINE

Fannie awoke to something warm and wet nibbling her ear. She fanned it away, then heard a throaty chuckle beside her. She opened her eyes and found Clay gazing down at her, a smile on his handsome face. Her heart skipped a beat at the sight of him.

"Good morning, sleepyhead," he said.

She blinked. "What time is it?"

"Almost ten."

"That late!" She made a move to get up, but he stopped her.

"Dad and Mandy are still in bed. I heard them come up sometime around dawn." His eyes impaled her as he reached up and stroked the line of her jaw. "There's no rush." He lowered his head and kissed her tenderly on the lips.

His intentions were clear. She was suddenly uneasy. "Clay, I—"

"Shhh. Don't talk. Just lie there and let me make you feel good." Even as he said it, he reached for the covers and brushed them aside.

Fannie felt exposed. His pajama shirt had ridden up during the night, falling at the waistband of her panties. She was suddenly thankful she wasn't wearing those god-awful cotton underwear that had caused Wilhemena to shudder. She didn't have much time to think about it. Clay captured her lips once more and sank his tongue deep inside. As he kissed her, he opened the buttons on the shirt one by one. Finally, he gazed down at her breasts, still flushed from sleep.

"So pretty," he said, reaching up to cup one. He lowered his head and took the cinnamon-colored nipple into his mouth, teasing it until it awoke to full erectness. Fannie closed her eyes, giving in to the sheer pleasure of having him suckle at her breast. His hair-roughened jaw grazed the tender skin and added to the delightful sensations. By the time he moved to the other breast, she could feel the heat building low in her belly. She squirmed on the bed. He moved one hand to her thigh and caressed her, then found his way inside her panties. He smiled softly when he found her wet.

Clay paused in his lovemaking only long enough to remove their clothes. As he continued kissing Fannie feverishly, he grasped her hand in his and moved it between his thighs, coaxing her to touch him. With very little direction, she began to stroke him until he was forced to stop her. He suddenly remembered the condom beside him and reached for it. If he waited another minute he might not care.

He entered her slowly, cautiously, closing his eyes when the sensation of being gripped so tightly was almost too much. He began to move, slowly at first, prodding her to follow. Too quickly, the pleasure became almost unbearable for both of them. Clay heard her gasp, felt her muscles contract around him, and knew she'd found release. She cried out softly, and he caught the sound with his lips as he plunged deeply inside her and shuddered in her arms.

Afterward, they were quiet, each caught up in their own thoughts. Clay, who'd never been one for making small talk before or after sex, wondered at the pensive frown on Fannie's face as she lay in his arms, staring at the ceiling.

"Okay, what?" he said when he could no longer resist.

She tipped her head so that she was looking at him. "Huh?"

"You've got something on your mind."

"That was . . . different from before," she said.

"Different?"

She nodded. "Is it always that good?"

Male pride made him puff up inside like a peacock. "If two people click, it usually gets better each time."

"And if they don't?"

He shrugged. "I guess it could be disappointing."

"Have you ever been disappointed with a woman?"

"Of course I have. I'm sure women have been disappointed with me." He grinned. "Not many I would think, but there's always that outside chance."

She elbowed him, and he laughed and hugged her closer. Finally, her look turned serious. "Were you disappointed with me?"

Her question surprised him, and his smile turned tender. "I could never be disappointed with you, Fannie. You're a passionate woman. I think once you realize I'm not out to hurt you, you'll be even more so."

"Hmmm." She raised up on one elbow and gazed down at him, a seductive smile playing across her lips. "Know what I think?" she said, but didn't wait for his reply. "I think I might like to try it again just to make sure."

He smiled. It was times like this he knew he was going to have one helluva time walking away from her when it was all over. "You got it, babe." He pulled her down for another kiss.

It was noon before they came downstairs, freshly showered and dressed for the day. They found Hyram and Mandy at the breakfast table. "Remind me never to play cards with your daughter again," the older man said. "The chef is mad at all of us for holding up breakfast. Claimed he made this fancy egg dish and had to throw it out when nobody showed."

"Oh, I'm sorry," Fannie said, feeling bad over the ruined food. Still, she was literally glowing inside and couldn't take her eyes off Clay. Every time their gazes met, he smiled that heart-stopping smile, and she was reminded of their lovemaking only an hour before. She wondered if anybody else could see the change in their relationship. Surely they were both being obvious as heck.

Once Clay had finished his first cup of coffee, he turned to Mandy. "How'd you like to go to Savannah and spend the night?" he said. "We could stay on the river. I know this great restaurant. Then—" He paused and his voice dropped an octave. "I could drive you to the airport Monday morning."

"That would be great," Mandy said. "I've never been to Savannah." She turned to Hyram. "What about you, Uncle Hy? Are you going?"

The older man shook his head. "Afraid not, dear. At my age traveling is more of a nuisance than a pleasure."

Clay gazed at the man quietly. His father had been such a powerful figure in his life, he'd never considered the fact that he was growing old. Was advancing age the reason for the changes in him?

They were on their way an hour later, riding in Hyram's Mercedes since Clay's car would have been too cramped for them. Mandy chatted almost nonstop during the hour-long drive while Fannie and Clay exchanged meaningful looks along the way.

Several uniformed doormen hurried up to greet them as they pulled onto the apron of a gleaming twelve-story hotel. All three made a joke of going through the revolving glass doors that led into an impressive lobby decorated in teal and white with tall vases of fuchsia-colored flowers. Clay checked in, and they were followed by yet another doorman rolling a metal cart bearing suitcases and hanging clothes. Although Clay and Fannie had brought only enough to see them through the night, Mandy had had to bring all her things for the trip back to Washington.

"I think you'll like your suite, Mr. Bodine," the doorman said as the elevator stopped at the tenth floor. "It's one of our finest. Actually, I'm surprised you were able to get it on such short notice. I understand the hotel is full."

Fannie looked at Clay in question as they got off the elevator, and he merely smiled in return. "How'd you do it?" she whispered.

He winked. "If you're willing to pay enough money, you can get anything you want."

She pondered his remark as they made their way down a teal-and-mauve hallway lined with flickering lights. "Maybe some things," she said. "But not *everything*."

He smiled as if he found her reply amusing and maybe just a little naive.

The suite was decorated in rose and dove-gray with a fully equipped kitchenette. The living room opened on either side to a bedroom. Mandy was given a room with double beds covered in rose-and-cream-striped comforters. Fannie sighed wistfully at the room she'd share with Clay. The mahogany king-size bed was draped in rose-colored satin and piled high with plump pillows.

"It's lovely," she said, running a hand across the comforter.

"*You're* lovely," Clay replied, watching her as she took in the room. The drapes were open behind her, spilling sunshine into the room and making her appear as though she were wearing a halo.

Fannie felt shy under his intense gaze. "I've never stayed in such a fine place. I suppose this is my week to play Cinderella."

He closed the distance between them and slipped his arm around her waist. "If you belonged to me, I'd see that you always had the best of everything."

"And you think that's what I want?"

"Isn't it?"

She pulled away. "I can think of a few other things I'd prefer in a relationship."

He crossed his arms and regarded her. "For example?"

She didn't hesitate. "Love. Deep devotion."

He thought it over. "I think most couples start out feeling that way. But those feelings die after a few years. Eventually, they learn to tolerate each other, but they stay together because of the kids or the house or some misplaced sense of loyalty. Then, before they know it, the kids are gone, and they've become total strangers."

Fannie sat on the edge of the bed. How sad that he'd grown up in such a household. She, on the other hand, had watched her father walk away from the woman he'd vowed to love and cherish. "Yes, I suppose some marriages are like that," she said regretfully. "But surely it doesn't have to be that way. I've seen couples come into the luncheonette who've been happily married for years."

He joined her on the bed and pushed her back, then gazed down at her face. "Is that what you want, Fannie? True love forever and ever?" He smiled. "Like in the fairy tales?"

She nodded. "Eventually. Once I have my own life in order. I don't think I can make someone else happy until I've accomplished my own goals."

He knew she was talking about her education and whatever other dreams she'd been forced to put on hold in her life. He put a finger under her chin and raised her head so that she was looking directly into his eyes. How could he make her understand that fulfilling her dreams was as important to him as it was to her?

"I don't know, Fannie. You've made me pretty happy these past couple of days. After this morning, all I can think about is holding you and making love to you." He kissed her tenderly on the lips. "I wouldn't think of standing in the way of your happiness."

He probably wouldn't do it on purpose, but it would happen just the same. Knowing Clay as she did, he would expect her to make him her top priority.

A knock at the adjoining door jolted them apart. "Are you guys going to make out all day?" Mandy said, grinning from ear to ear. "Or are we going to do something fun?"

Clay frowned, grabbed a throw pillow, and threw it at her. She ducked and it landed in the next room. "Can't you see I'm busy?" he said, pretending to be annoyed. "How do you expect me to sweep Fannie off her feet when you keep interrupting?"

"I thought we were going sight-seeing."

Clay glanced at Fannie, who was smiling up at him, and he knew the only sight-seeing he wanted to do concerned her. He sighed and pushed himself into a sitting position. "Okay, okay," he mumbled, deciding there would be plenty of time for that later. "Where do you want to go first?"

"I want to look in those little shops along the

river," Mandy said, obviously impatient to be on her way. She hurried across the room, grabbed Fannie's hand, and tugged. "Come on, let's go!"

"Wait, I have to repair my lipstick," she said.

"You wouldn't have to keep doing that if Clay would stop kissing you." She was forced to dodge another throw pillow from Clay.

Laughing softly, Fannie stood, then stepped into the bathroom long enough to check her hair and apply lipstick. "Okay, I'm ready," she announced. "I certainly don't want to be the one to keep this group waiting."

The three of them entered the elevator once again, this time headed for the lobby where a man in a dark suit played soft music on a gleaming black baby grand piano. Several couples lounged nearby on overstuffed furniture, sipping cocktails and chatting softly among themselves.

The sun was still high in the sky, but a gentle breeze coming off the river made it pleasant. They passed a craft store, where handmade cradles and high chairs held expensive porcelain dolls with human hair and exquisite lace nightgowns and frilly gingham dresses. Fannie's attention was drawn to a newborn model tucked beneath a patchwork quilt in a handmade crib.

"Look out," Mandy told Clay, nudging him slightly as Fannie gazed wistfully at the baby doll. "Next thing you know she'll be wanting a baby."

Fannie's eyes clouded. "Don't worry," she

said. "I'm not about to bring a child into this world until I'm one hundred percent prepared."

Clay grabbed her arm, and they walked to the next shop. The smell of fresh coffee and pecan pie wafted through the open doorway. Although it took a great deal of willpower, they passed the shop and stepped inside the next one, The Christmas Shoppe, as it was called, where artificial trees were adorned with fake white birds and gold angels holding harps. Red satin bows had been tied to another tree that had been sprayed with artificial snow, and tiny elves played among the branches. Lights flickered and bells sounded various Christmas tunes.

"Wow, it's Christmastime all year-round here," Mandy exclaimed.

Fannie smiled and nodded, thinking of how different her holidays must've been from Clay's and Mandy's. They'd had very little money to buy gifts, especially after her father had left. Nevertheless, Christmas had been a special time. If they couldn't afford a big turkey with all the trimmings, they could at least buy a hen and make do with vegetables from the garden. Fannie's last Christmas with her mother had been a happy one and that's all that had mattered.

They left the shop a few minutes later and followed Mandy into a T-shirt store. Clay purchased a variety of T-shirts, some of them bearing the words "Welcome to Savannah," others with cute but naughty sayings like "Hot Stuff" on the front of them. He handed that particular one to Fannie and whispered in her ear.

"After this morning I think you've earned it."

"Never mind," she mumbled, her cheeks flaming, hoping Mandy hadn't heard from where she stood.

They ate dinner in a restaurant Clay recommended. He ordered a dozen raw oysters and discovered Mandy was crazy about them. Fannie sat and watched them eat their fill, turning down all offers to try one. Once their dinner arrived, she surprised them by eating close to an entire pound of steamed shrimp.

The shops were still open when they made their way back to the hotel, all three holding hands and talking. Fannie couldn't help but enjoy the feel of Clay's hand, big and warm and protective, around hers. She wondered at the giddiness she felt inside. Surely it was the glass of wine she'd had before dinner making her feel that way.

"Did you know we have pay TV in the room?" Mandy said, almost skipping down the thickly carpeted hallway. "What d'you say we sit up all night and watch it?"

"Aren't you at all tired after sitting up last night?" Fannie said laughingly.

"I'm too excited to sleep. I know, let's go swimming first. You brought your bathing suit, didn't you?"

Fannie nodded. She'd brought Wilhemena's bathing suit, but she hadn't tried it on yet.

"I'm game," Clay said.

Fifteen minutes later they were back on the elevator in search of the swimming pool. They found an enclosed Olympic-size pool surrounded by lounge chairs. Off to one side was a gurgling hot tub. Mandy dropped her towel on the concrete floor and dove in.

"I'm going to miss her like crazy when she's gone," Fannie said as she watched her daughter swim to the other side of the pool. "I can't stand the thought of letting her go."

"Maybe you won't have to."

She gave him a funny look. "Of course I have to. She's not my child. I gave her up, remember?"

"She can still visit."

"Not if she's living on the other side of the world."

"You've heard of airplanes?"

She sighed. "Clay, you know as well as I do that I wouldn't be able to afford the plane fare." She shook her head sadly as Mandy began doing laps. "I should never have let her go in the first place."

"Don't start that again. Haven't you berated yourself enough?"

"But look what I missed out on."

Mandy paused at the shallow end of the pool.

"Aren't you guys coming in?" she asked. "The water's perfect."

Without warning, Clay took off, jumped high and tucked his legs beneath him, splashing Fannie once he landed in the water. She shrieked as the cold water hit her. She was not one of those who could dive in and be done with it. She had to acclimate herself to the water. She started down the steps, slowly and one at a time, while Mandy and Clay laughed and cajoled and splashed. Once in, Clay began a wicked game of dunking the two of them. Finally, the girls teamed up and shoved him under the water, but he managed to grab a firm hold on each one and hold them under until they came up coughing and sputtering.

The hotel room was cold when they entered more than an hour later, wrapped in fluffy over-size towels they'd had to sign for at the pool. "I'm taking a warm shower," Mandy announced in a shivery voice as she made for her room.

"Me too," Fannie muttered, heading in the opposite direction. She hurried into the bathroom, stripped off her suit, and stepped into the tiled shower. She adjusted the water temperature and turned on the nozzle. The warm spray took the chill off her skin immediately.

"Scoot over," a masculine voice said, climbing into the shower behind her.

Fannie was so taken by surprise, she almost slipped. He reached out and steadied her. Her mouth flew open and filled with water. She coughed and spit it out, then tried to cover herself. "I didn't hear you come in."

He chuckled. "You weren't supposed to. Stop hiding, Fannie. I've already seen everything you've got."

She frowned. "Don't you ever wait to be invited?"

"Never. Now, stop fussing and let me wash your back." He took the soap and washcloth from her hands and worked up a lather. "Turn around."

Fannie sighed and did as she was told, offering him her backside. It wasn't an easy task. Living with her mother who'd been unbearably modest even in front of her daughter, she wasn't accustomed to exposing any part of her body. She stood frozen in place while Clay washed her back, each hip, and finally her thighs and legs, slipping into crevices that made her heart beat faster.

"Now, that wasn't so bad, was it?" he said. "Turn around so I can get the other side."

"Clay—"

"Hurry up. Mandy's going to wonder what's taking us so long."

Fannie presented her front. Once again, Clay worked up a generous lather and soaped her all over, spending an inordinate amount of time on her breasts. By the time he moved to her belly, her nipples were straining. Finally, he moved his hand to the reddish-gold tuft at her thighs. It was all Fannie could do to keep from pressing herself against his hand. Just as she was allowing herself to give in to the pleasure, he slid his soapy fingers inside and worked them in and out. His index finger sought and found the little bud that quivered for attention. Fannie closed her eyes and leaned against him as he brought her to climax. She cried out softly as waves of pleasure hit her, one after the other, each building with an intensity that left her trembling afterward.

They found a solemn-eyed Mandy on the sofa in the sitting room when they entered later, Clay in his pajama bottoms and Fannie wearing a bathrobe. "Why so glum?" Clay asked the girl, then noted the blank television set. "I thought you were going to sit up all night watching the latest movies."

"I just called home," Mandy said. "My parents were called out of the country tonight for some top secret international emergency. They supposedly tried to reach me back at the house, then here at the hotel, but I was out."

Fannie took a seat beside her daughter. She could see the girl was near tears. "Where are they going?"

Mandy shrugged. "Who knows? When the White House calls, my father goes without question. This time my mother went with him."

Fannie glanced at Clay then back at the girl. It didn't make sense that her adoptive parents would make those kind of arrangements without seeing to their daughter's welfare first. "Who will take care of you while they're gone?"

"My aunt Rhea." The girl looked miserable at the thought. "You don't suppose—" She paused and looked at Fannie, her expression hopeful. "You don't suppose I could come back home with you." When Fannie hesitated, she went on quickly. "It's only for a few more days. A week at the most. These things are usually resolved quickly and quietly."

Fannie was at a loss as to what to do. She turned troubled eyes to Clay. "I don't know—"

"Of course you can come back with us, Mandy," he interrupted. "You're family. You're welcome anytime."

Fannie couldn't hide her appreciation. The fact that Clay was so willing to take her daughter into his house touched her deeply. She knew Hyram would be just as eager. "We'd love to have you, sweetie," she said. "You'll have to cancel your flight. Would you like me to call your aunt?"

Mandy shook her head quickly. "I'd better do it. If she's going to fuss, I'd rather she fuss at me." She got up from the sofa, a look of immense relief on her face. "I'll make the call in my room if you don't mind."

Fannie waited until they were alone before she said anything. "Thank you, Clay. You didn't have to do that."

He shrugged. "What was I going to do, send

the kid back when it's obvious she doesn't want to go?"

She was thoughtful. "Don't you think that's a bit strange?" she asked. "For her adoptive parents to pack up and leave at a moment's notice?"

"Our government has been known to act strangely at times. Her father must be pretty high up on the ladder if he takes orders directly from the White House. I had no idea he was so important."

They were still discussing the situation when the bedroom door opened a few minutes later and Mandy stepped through. "Is everything okay?" Fannie asked.

The girl offered her a sheepish smile. "Frankly, I think Aunt Rhea was relieved. She said she'd relay the message to my parents. When and *if* she sees them again."

Fannie and Clay exchanged anxious looks. "What's that supposed to mean?" Fannie asked.

"These missions are sometimes dangerous," Mandy replied casually. "Surely you know that. My parents could be killed."

Fannie's hand flew to her chest. "What a terrible thought!"

The girl reclaimed her seat on the sofa. "Terrible, maybe, but true. Why do you think I dread leaving the country once school's out? You know how unstable everything is in the Middle East. By the way, I changed my ticket with no sweat."

"You're going to the Middle East?" Clay

asked, more concerned about that than her plane ticket.

Mandy glanced away quickly. "I wasn't supposed to tell. Please don't let on that you know."

Once again, Fannie sought Clay's gaze, then shook her head, unable to take everything in. This was not the time to talk about it. She reached for Mandy's hand and squeezed it. "You look exhausted, honey. Why don't you go to bed. We'll talk more tomorrow."

"You're right, I am tired," Mandy confessed, then offered her a brief hug. "I guess I worry too much, but I can't help it. It's no fun wondering if your family is going to make it out of some foreign country alive. Especially with all this terrorism going on." She stood and made her way out of the room without another word.

"This is insane," Clay said after a moment. "How long has the poor kid been living like this?"

Fannie shook her head once more. "I have no idea. Everything was kept hush-hush at the adoption. Nobody told me her father was a big-shot government agent who'd constantly be putting his family's life at risk."

"It's all so . . . unbelievable," he said.

"And scary. Clay, I can't let them take Mandy to the Middle East. Lord, I can't believe Americans are still allowed to travel to that part of the world. Even big-shot government agents. Don't they know how dangerous it is? Surely there's something I can do to prevent it. If you ask me, I think it's high time I spoke with Mandy's adoptive parents."

He saw the fire in her eyes and knew she would go to all lengths to protect her daughter. "What'll you say?"

She hesitated. "I'm not sure. Maybe I should threaten legal action if they take her out of the country. Surely there's *something* I can do."

Clay pondered it. "I'll talk to my lawyer first thing in the morning and see what he says. In the meantime, try to stop worrying and let's get some sleep."

Fannie was glad Clay didn't push her into making love. Her thoughts were so scattered at the moment, she wasn't sure she would have been able to concentrate. All she could think of was her poor daughter and the possibility of her going to a dangerous country. Her adoptive parents needed to have their heads examined for even thinking such a thing.

Clay could see that Fannie had a lot on her mind as he lay beside her, holding her against him, his legs tucked beneath hers. His own thoughts ran rampant as well. Something didn't seem right about all Mandy had told them. He was determined to find out what was really going on. He fell asleep long after he heard Fannie's steady breathing beside him.

❧———————————❧

"I've been fired," Fannie told Clay the following morning as he sipped his first cup of coffee.

He was only half awake, watching in fascination as Fannie braided her long hair and fixed a rubber band near the bottom to hold it. "What happened?"

"I called my boss at the Griddle and Grill this morning. Told him I was still sick. He said Wilhemena told him I had mono."

"Oh, jeez." Clay rolled his eyes and would have laughed had she not looked so distraught over the fact.

"From what I gathered of their conversation, he was grilling her as to why it was taking me so long to get over a simple bug. She obviously couldn't think of any other explanation.

He noted how clean and fresh she looked in white jeans and a navy pullover, and he hated that she'd managed to shower and dress without waking him. "So he fired you because you have mononucleosis?"

"He said he couldn't be without a counter person for that long. Do you realize what this means?"

"That you're without a job?"

"Not to mention all my benefits. That's one of the reasons I put up with him all these years. I had a great insurance plan."

"You'll find something else," he said. "You ask me, that was a dead-end position anyway."

She shot him a look of annoyance. "Sometimes you do what you have to in order to pay your bills."

Clay set his coffee cup on the night table and stood. "I didn't mean it to sound like that," he said, closing the distance between them. He reached for her, encircling her waist with his arms. She smelled like a summer garden. "All I meant was—" He paused to gather his thoughts. "I care a helluva lot about you, Fannie. I don't like the idea of you working so hard, standing on your feet all day over a hot grill, dealing with cranky customers. And I don't appreciate your boss acting like such a jerk, especially after all the years you've put in. I want more for you. Is that such a crime?"

"I want more for myself, Clay," she said, touched that he cared so much. "But that's going to take time. I don't really have that many job skills—"

"That's bull and you know it. You've spent half your life caring for a sick person, not to mention handling the cooking and cleaning and bill paying. It takes a lot of ability to do all that. Stop underestimating yourself."

She pulled away. "If you're suggesting I get a job in a hospital or nursing home, forget it. I don't want to be around sick people any more than I have to." She sighed. "Just don't worry about it. I'll find another job."

Once again he reached for her, noting with

surprise how her unhappiness affected him so deeply. "Let me help you. Do you realize I've never really helped another human being in all my life? Pretty sad, isn't it? To be so self-absorbed."

"Help me what?" she asked, her brow wrinkling.

"Let me give you some money to tide you over."

"Haven't we been through this before? I don't want your stupid money."

"You can even pay me back once you get on your feet. You let me know what kind of monthly payments you can live with and—"

Fannie put a finger to his lips and silenced him. "Before you call the Red Cross on me, let me tell you something. I do have a savings account I can draw on. I'm not totally indigent."

He kissed the tip of her finger and moved it. "You know what I think?" he said, then went on without waiting for an answer. "I think you'd sooner starve than let me help you. Is it just me, or is it any man?"

"You're being silly. Of course I'd accept your help if I needed it. But right now I don't."

Clay wondered if she would ever need him for anything.

Mandy seemed delighted to be going back home with them. As they ate breakfast from an elaborate buffet set up in the hotel dining area, she read aloud from various brochures what the historic town had to offer.

"I wish we could stay another day," she said wistfully. "There's so many things to do and see in this town."

"Maybe we *can* stay another day," Clay said, draining the last of his coffee.

Fannie turned to him. "Don't you have to work?"

He shrugged. "I've got a couple of appointments, but I can probably put them off until the middle of the week. Tell you what. Why don't you two finish your breakfast and I'll go back to the room and make some calls." He winked at Mandy and slid from the booth.

"You're very lucky," Mandy said as she watched him go. "To have such an adoring husband."

Fannie shifted uncomfortably in the booth. "Yes, I suppose I am." At the same time, she couldn't help but wonder how much of Clay's devoted husband act was being put on for Mandy's benefit. How would she deal with it when Mandy went back and they were forced to go their separate ways? She was thankful she had been given a few more days.

TEN

Two days later, Clay arrived home from work and found Fannie looking through the classified section of the newspaper. "Still searching for a job?" he asked, pouring a glass of lemonade from a frosty pitcher that someone had brought in on a tray.

Fannie folded the paper. "The job market in Culpepper is rather lean these days," she said. "But I'm sure I'll find something in the Sunday edition." She smiled but couldn't help noticing he looked distracted.

He nodded and took a sip of the drink, then ended up draining the glass as though he'd been thirstier than he'd thought. He wiped his mouth. "We need to talk. Where's Mandy?"

"Out riding." She arched one brow. "What's wrong? You sound so serious."

He set his glass down, crossed the room, and

closed the door. "I heard from my lawyer today," he said when he returned. "Regarding Mandy."

Fannie felt the hairs stand up on the back of her neck at his tone. "And?"

He sighed heavily. "I don't quite know how to tell you this, Fannie, but the girl has been lying to us all along."

She offered him a blank look. "Lying? About what?"

"You know how she led us to believe her adoptive father was some kind of government agent? Well, none of that's true. Her father *did* work for the government, but not in that capacity. His job wasn't dangerous by any means."

Fannie frowned. "But why would Mandy tell us something like that?"

He held up one hand. "Wait. It gets worse. Her adoptive parents were killed last year by a drunk driver."

"Oh, Clay, no!"

"Mandy was in the backseat and saw the whole thing. Fortunately, her injuries weren't serious."

Fannie shook her head, not because she didn't believe it but because she didn't *want* to believe it. She didn't want to think of her poor daughter going through such an ordeal. "Where has she been living all this time?"

"With her aunt Rhea, the woman she told us about. The woman is somewhat elderly, doesn't really want the responsibility of a teenager, but she promised Mandy's adoptive parents she'd look after the girl if anything ever happened to them. She feels obligated to keep that promise no matter what."

"Clay, how did you find all this out? And so fast?"

"My lawyer has a lawyer friend in Washington who knows this crackerjack private investigator. This P.I. talked to the sister's neighbor who was only too happy to give him the rundown on the situation once he flashed a few bills in her face. Now, we get to the really bad news."

Fannie winced. "I'm almost afraid to ask at this point."

"Mandy has run away."

She gasped. "Run away!"

"She obviously couldn't stand living with her aunt any longer."

Fannie stood and walked to the window, glancing out for any sign of her daughter. She didn't see her. Perhaps she was already on her way back to the house so she could clean up for dinner. "This is all so unbelievable," she said. "Why would Mandy do something like this? And why did she tell us all these fantastic stories about moving to the Middle East and such?"

She looked at him. "The letter," she whispered, more to herself than him. "Mandy was the one who wrote it." When Clay merely looked at her as though he didn't know what she was talking about, she went on. "I received a letter from

Mandy's adoptive mother, or at least that's who I thought it was from. Although she informed me she'd given Mandy permission to visit, she made it clear she was very hurt and left me feeling the less they heard from me the better. Which is why I didn't respond," she said. "Mandy was obviously counting on that."

"She certainly did a clever job of fooling us," Clay said. "Makes one wonder how long she's been planning it."

There was a knock at the door. Mandy poked her head through. Clay and Fannie turned, and the expressions on their faces must've startled her. "I'm sorry for interrupting," she said. "I just wanted to let you know I was back. I didn't fall off the horse, and she didn't throw me or drag me or kick me like you were afraid she would. And I stayed near the house too. I hope soon you'll let me ride within shouting distance."

"Please come in," Fannie said gently, in no mood for joking. "We need to talk to you."

"Uh-oh. Did the stable boy complain about the way I was handling the horses or something? I'm very good with animals, you know. I wouldn't do anything to—"

"It's not about the horses," Fannie said quickly.

The girl came farther into the room, checking the seat of her jeans before she sat down on the sofa. She poured a glass of lemonade and took a hefty drink.

Fannie clasped her hands together and regarded the girl with a worried frown. She could not fathom why Mandy had lied so unabashedly, and she wondered if the accident had left her with deep emotional scars.

"Clay and I have been so worried about you that we decided to do some checking in Washington." She didn't want to put the blame on Clay alone and have Mandy resent him. She saw a look of horror cross her daughter's face, and she knew the information Clay had received was true. "We've discovered you haven't been completely honest with us, Mandy. Would you mind telling us why?"

The girl set her glass down. "You found out about my parents?"

"Yes." Fannie joined her on the sofa and took her hand. "We're very sorry, Mandy," she said, her voice thick with emotion. "So very sorry."

Tears sprang to the girl's eyes, and she glanced away quickly. "It's been a year now, but it's still hard to talk about."

"Why didn't you tell me they'd died? And why did you tell us that bizarre tale about your father being a government agent and moving you to the Middle East?"

Mandy refused to look at her. "I wanted to tell you the truth, but I was afraid you'd feel sorry for me and insist I come live with you. I didn't want you to invite me out of pity. Not after you went through all that trouble to get rid of me."

Fannie felt as though she'd been stabbed in the heart. She could feel her own eyes burning with tears. At the window, Clay was quiet. She wished he would say something, tell her how to handle this.

"Of course I want you, Mandy," she said softly. "I've *always* wanted you, from the moment I knew you were growing inside of me. I gave you up because I couldn't bear to bring you into a life of poverty. Please don't hate me for that."

The girl literally threw herself in Fannie's arms as a giant sob escaped her throat. Fannie embraced her tightly. "I knew I shouldn't have told you all that crazy stuff about my father," she said. "I was hoping if you thought he had this really dangerous job, you wouldn't let me go back. It would be your choice not to send me back, you see. You wouldn't have felt as if you were forced to act because I had no place else to go." She sniffed. "Okay, so it doesn't make complete sense, but it sounded good at the time I was planning the whole thing."

"But didn't you think I'd check out your story first?"

The girl shrugged. "I guess I didn't really think about it. I was desperate. All I knew was I didn't want to have to go back to Washington and live with my aunt Rhea." Mandy raised tear-stained cheeks to her. "She's almost seventy years old, for Pete's sake, and she's a religious fanatic. Everything I do is a sin as far as she's concerned.

I've already told you about the school she put me in where I have to wear old-lady clothes. I'm not allowed to go out with my friends, and heaven forbid if a boy calls the house."

Mandy paused and glanced at Clay, then back at Fannie. "Do you realize I'm thirteen years old and not even allowed to shave my legs?"

Clay moved away from the window and shoved his hands deep into his pockets. "Your aunt obviously loves you very much, Mandy. She's got everybody in Washington looking for you right now. It wouldn't surprise me if your picture started showing up on all the milk cartons." He paused. "I understand her health isn't good."

Fresh tears filled Mandy's eyes and splattered down her cheeks like raindrops. "I never meant to hurt her. I only wanted out. I was desperate."

"How did you find me?" Fannie asked. "Everything was kept so quiet at the adoption."

"It wasn't easy," the girl confessed, "but when Aunt Rhea was cleaning out my parents' things, she came upon this old wooden cradle—"

"The one my father made," Fannie said, then glanced at Clay. "My father used to build furniture in his spare time. Actually, he was very good at it and tried to start up his own business once, but it fell through the way everything else he attempted did." She looked at Mandy. "I'd forgotten I'd sent the cradle with you."

"As well as some knitted blankets," Mandy

said. "My mother kept them all. Anyway, your father had signed his name and address in the wood, plus the date. I would never have been able to make it out after all these years if I hadn't sprinkled ashes from the fireplace in it the way I once saw someone do on television. After that, I just started making telephone calls."

"How long have you known?" Fannie asked.

"Almost since the accident. But I had to work up my nerve to contact you." She paused and looked embarrassed. "And I had to come up with some kind of plan. I had no way of knowing whether you'd even want to see me."

Fannie hugged the girl against her for a long moment, wishing she could have somehow spared her all the pain she'd been through. "Oh, Mandy, I wish you'd come to me in the beginning."

She shook her head. "I couldn't. Not right away. I was too upset over losing my parents."

Fannie pulled away. "You know you're going to have to call your aunt," she said gently. "You can't let her worry about you. Especially when she has all those health problems."

"I *can't* call her," Mandy said. "She'll never forgive me. And what if she sends the police for me? What if they handcuff me and—" She was getting worked up. "Just let me stay here," the girl pleaded. "Please. I won't cause you any trouble."

The idea sounded tempting to Fannie, who

had no desire to send her daughter back to live in those conditions. "What do you think your aunt would say to that?" she asked.

"She'd probably make me come home out of spite. She doesn't want me. I'm a headache to her, but she promised my mother she'd take care of me. Asking her to break a promise would be like asking her to dance naked in front of the White House."

They were all quiet for a moment. Finally, Clay spoke. "Mandy, why don't you go ahead and get cleaned up for dinner. I'd like to talk to Fannie alone."

The girl looked from one to the other, shoulders slumped, her expression one of total desolation. She rose from the sofa and made her way quietly to the door, then paused before opening it. "I'm sorry for causing all this trouble," she said. "I never meant to hurt anyone. Maybe Aunt Rhea's right. Maybe I really am bad." She let herself out the door before either of them could respond.

Neither Clay nor Fannie said anything right away. Finally, Fannie spoke. "I don't think I like Aunt Rhea very much."

"You and me both. What are we going to do?" he asked.

She glanced at him. He'd said *we*. She wanted to assure him it wasn't his problem and she would handle it as best she could. "I'll call her before dinner. That's all I know to do. Then, I'll drive Mandy back to Washington personally and—"

"Just like that?" he asked. "Without a fight?"

"I don't have any legal right to the girl, Clay. All I can hope for at this point is that her aunt, as strict as she sounds, doesn't throw Mandy in some juvenile hall or something. At the same time, I'm going to do everything in my power to become friends with the woman. Whether I like her or not," she added. "Maybe I can convince her to cut Mandy some slack. I'm hoping in time she'll let the girl visit me. Once I earn the woman's trust, who knows what'll happen. She's old. Her health isn't good. Maybe after a while she'll let Mandy stay. By then I'd have my degree, and I could make a decent living for the two of us." She knew she was rambling, searching for answers.

He scowled at the idea. "That could take years. You heard it for yourself, the kid is miserable. I don't like to think of her having to live there any longer than she already has."

Fannie felt the same way but knew if she dwelled on it she'd fall apart. She couldn't stand the thought of Mandy being unhappy. "What would you have me do, Clay?" she said sharply. "Have you forgotten my situation? I'm without a job, I don't have an education, and my house is falling down over my head. I'm back in the same boat I was in when I let Mandy go. Her aunt's not going to let me have her. And if I don't take her back, the woman will probably have me picked up for kidnapping."

He stood and closed the distance between them with long purposeful strides. "You don't have to be in that position," he said. "Not anymore." He paused. "I'm crazy about you, Fannie. I'm so crazy about you, I don't think of anything else all day. And I'm crazy about your daughter." He slipped his arms around her waist.

Fannie was confused. She shook her head slightly as though hoping it would jog something inside and what he was saying would make sense and have purpose. "This is all wonderful news, Clay, but what has this got to do with helping Mandy?"

"Marry me, babe. We'll work this out together."

ELEVEN

At first she thought she'd misunderstood. Marry him? No, surely not. Clay Bodine wasn't the marrying kind. "I don't think I heard you right."

"You heard me just fine," he said. "We'll contact Mandy's aunt, then stall while we wait for the marriage license. We'll be good and married by the time we face the woman."

She was stunned. That was the only reason she could explain why her mouth was still open. She sat down. Married? She looked at him. "But you don't love me," she said, knowing how he felt about love and marriage and family. "Why would you even consider such a thing?"

He sat down beside her. "What *is* love, Fannie? I'm certainly closer to you than I've ever been to anyone else. I can't wait to see you at the end of the day, and when we make love—" He paused and shook his head, unable to describe what it meant to him. "And I enjoy the hell out of waking up next to you in the morning. Unless I'm mistaken, I think you feel pretty much the same about me."

He was right, of course. She had grown very close to him over the past week. In fact, what she was feeling was dangerously close to love. But how could they commit themselves to a long-term relationship when they weren't absolutely certain? And what about her goals? Would she have to continue to put them off?

"I know what you're thinking," Clay said. "You're thinking Mandy and I will interfere with your college plans."

"I suppose that's pretty selfish of me," she told him. "Mandy's my daughter. Her happiness comes first."

He shook his head. "It doesn't have to be that way, Fannie. You can have your family *and* your education. You won't have to work in some hash house to make ends meet. There'll be plenty of time for your studies *and* us."

He was telling her he'd support her. *And* her daughter. "What's in it for you?" she blurted out without thinking. She regretted it the moment she said it, but she had to know.

He didn't try to hide the fact that she'd offended him. "Can't you accept something without always suspecting the motives behind it?" he asked.

"Sorry, but it's a habit of mine. Only last

week you were accusing me of being a gold digger, of having designs on your father."

"I made a mistake. I'm sorry. I guess the experience with my stepmother left a bad taste in my mouth." He paused and gazed at her for a long moment. "I suppose I do have my own reasons for doing this," he said. "You and Mandy have shown me how nice it is to be part of a family again. I haven't felt that way in a long time. Frankly, I don't remember when I last did, but it's a helluva lot nicer coming home at the end of the day when there's somebody waiting who gives a damn about you."

"What about your relationship with your father? You know he'd give anything to have you back here."

"I'll have to deal with him in my own way. Something has changed him. I don't know what it is, but I like the man he has become. As for where we'll live, we could stay here for a couple of months just to see how it works. As long as he doesn't try to interfere with us—"

Fannie wondered if Hyram would ever tell Clay about the heart attack and how close to death he'd come. Perhaps in time he would, once they'd put the past behind them. Or maybe Clay didn't have to know now that Hyram was on the mend and following doctor's orders. Maybe it was good enough that the two men were working toward a better relationship.

"I don't think you have to worry about your

father getting in our way," she said. "He wants you home so badly, he'll be on his best behavior."

Clay took her hand and gazed at her longingly. "So what do you say? Will you marry me? That way we could all be together."

She hesitated. "What if it doesn't work?"

He shook his head. "Always the optimist, aren't you?" he said, sarcasm slipping into his voice.

"I have to think about the future. Especially if there's a chance I'll be reunited with my daughter." The thought that she might was almost more than she could comprehend at the moment.

"Okay, let me say this. I'm going to do everything humanly possible to make it work between us. On the outside chance it doesn't, I'll see that you and Mandy are provided for."

She bristled. "I thought I'd made it plain I don't need your money."

"Please let me finish. I will provide for you until you earn your degree and find a job. As your husband, it's the least I can do. But I don't want to think along those lines. I'm not planning on failing in this."

"You'll go with us to Washington?"

He nodded. "We'll face Mandy's aunt together. Once she sees how much we care for each other, as well as her niece, she'll be only too glad to let her go."

"You sound confident."

"I have a way with elderly women. You should have seen me around my grandmother. Had her wrapped around my little finger. Mandy's aunt will be putty in my hands."

He had a way with younger women as well, Fannie told herself. All he had to do was walk into a room to send her into a tailspin. Nevertheless, she didn't feel so cocky where Rhea Turnbull, Mandy's guardian, was concerned. "What if she doesn't go for it?"

"We go to court. Whatever it takes to get Mandy."

"You've gotten attached to her."

He shrugged. "She's not a bad kid."

Fannie suspected that was as close as he was going to get to admitting his feelings for the girl. Why was it so hard for Clay to open up? Was it because of his father? He could show he cared in a hundred little ways, but to actually open up and say the words seemed difficult for him.

"Do I need to give you my answer right this minute?" she asked. "Can I have some time to think it through?"

"Don't take too long. We still have to apply for a marriage license and wait twenty-four hours afterward."

She nodded. It wasn't the sort of marriage proposal she'd expected to receive from a man who wished to spend the rest of his life with her; certainly it was nothing like one of those corny late shows where the prospective groom got down on bended knee and asked for the woman's hand. But then nothing else in her life had been very predictable either.

That didn't mean it couldn't work. She loved him. Perhaps in time he'd grow to love her. "Yes," she said at last. "I'll marry you."

Fannie awoke at dawn the day of the ceremony after a fitful night. She slipped out of bed, taking great care not to wake Clay, and hurried across the hall to her daughter's room. Mandy was sleeping soundly, one hand tucked beneath her cheek. Fannie thought she looked like an angel, and once again her heart swelled with love. The thought of losing her almost sucked her breath away. But there was no way of getting around it, she had to take the girl back. After talking to her aunt two days before, it was clear the woman wouldn't hesitate to send the authorities after her niece. It didn't matter that the girl had lost her family only a year earlier or that she was terribly unhappy in her present situation, no excuses would be accepted.

Fannie shook her daughter gently. "Wake up, Mandy," she whispered. When the girl opened her eyes, Fannie smiled. "Get up, sleepyhead. I want to take you for a drive."

Mandy glanced toward the darkened window. "You mean *now?*"

The girl was still half asleep as Fannie led her

to one of three garage doors on the side of the house and opened it. Her clunker was still where Clay had parked it more than a week before, sitting in the dark like a forgotten friend. She saw the curious expression on her daughter's face and chuckled. "You ever ridden in a car without air-conditioning?" she asked.

The girl shook her head. "Whose car is it?"

"Mine. Go around on the other side and get in," Fannie told her. "You'll have to reach inside to open the door because the handle on the outside doesn't work."

Mandy nodded and did as she was told. She didn't say anything until Fannie had started the engine and backed out. "What's going on, Mom?"

It was the first time her daughter had referred to her as her mother, and it startled Fannie so badly, she almost ran off the gravel drive. She glanced at her daughter, then back at the road. She didn't want to see the disappointment on Mandy's face when she told her what needed to be said.

"I lied to you, honey," she said after a moment. "About who I am and what I am."

The girl simply nodded. "I know."

Fannie slammed on the brakes. The car skidded to a halt, and the engine died. "You do?" She blinked several times, unable to read the look on Mandy's face. "Why didn't you say something?"

She shrugged. "I figured you'd tell me the

truth when you were ready. Besides—" She paused and grinned. "I wasn't exactly honest myself, telling you and Clay all that stuff about my dad being a government agent. I can't believe I came up with something so dumb. I'm surprised you believed it."

"We didn't have any reason not to," Fannie told her. She sighed and offered her daughter a meek smile. "I'm going to sound very motherly saying this, but I guess it all goes back to the truth being the best policy and all, huh?" She chuckled. "I wonder if the person responsible for that saying got himself in the same kind of mess we did?"

Mandy laughed. "Could be." Her gaze softened. "I like it when you sound like a mother."

Fannie was so touched, she feared she might cry. She blinked several times as she restarted the engine.

They drove a distance in silence, each of them caught up in her own thoughts. Mandy knew they were leaving for Washington that afternoon and she would ultimately have to face her aunt, but she'd said very little about it. It was obvious she wasn't looking forward to returning. Fannie had not discussed the strategy she and Clay had planned, simply because she had no idea what to expect from the woman, and she didn't want to get Mandy's hopes up.

Her house looked the same when Fannie pulled into the drive and parked, battered and so badly mildewed in places that it was starting to rot. The sagging, lopsided porch looked as though it had been hit by a fierce wind, and she'd lost count of the many places the roof leaked.

Fannie turned off the engine and sat quietly for a moment, remembering the years she'd spent inside that house, good and bad. "Well, this is it," she said, and heard the apology in her voice. When her daughter didn't say anything, she went on. "Actually, the outside is much better than the inside. Needs painting, of course. I never had the time or the money."

Mandy looked thoughtful. "You grew up here?"

"Yep." She made it sound as if it were no big deal when it really had been. She had hated the poverty and the sickness and the feeling that she was all alone in the world. She had hated watching her mother deteriorate, of getting her hopes up when she went into remission, only to have them sink low when the woman got sick again. She sighed. "Come on, let's go in."

Mandy followed her up a cracked walk to the porch and waited while Fannie unlocked the door. Once inside, she studied her surroundings thoughtfully. "Has it always been this gloomy?"

Fannie was surprised at how dreary the place looked. After spending time in the Bodine mansion, she thought it resembled a tomb. "I guess I was used to it."

Mandy walked toward the back of the house

to the crudely designed kitchen. She sat down at the table and waited for Fannie to do the same. "Why'd you want to show me this place?"

Taking the chair right next to her, Fannie clasped her hands together on the battered wooden table. "I was hoping you'd understand why I let you go, Mandy. I didn't want you to have to live here and be ashamed of having friends over. I never really had girlfriends while I was growing up because I didn't want to invite them over. Also, my mother never felt well enough for company."

"Clay said your father abandoned you?"

Fannie nodded. "He said he couldn't live around all that sickness." She sat there for a moment. "He really tried hard in the beginning, coming up with all kinds of get-rich schemes." She chuckled. "Nothing came of them. The only thing he was really good at was woodworking. But you already know that. What most folks didn't know was each piece took hours of pains-taking work. They didn't want to pay what the pieces were worth so he stopped doing it."

"What was wrong with your mother?"

"She had multiple sclerosis. She was sick for a long time before she died last year with compli-cations. I think she lost the will to live."

"You miss her, don't you?" Mandy said softly.

"She was my best friend. I used to get mad at her for not fighting harder. Some people live a lot longer with the disease. I think she gave up the minute my father walked out the door. I think she lived a lot longer than she wanted to."

Mandy seemed to ponder everything she'd been told. Finally, she propped her elbows on the table, linked her fingers together, and rested her chin there. She gazed at Fannie for a moment. "Look, I just want you to know—" She paused and her bottom lip trembled. Tears glistened in her eyes. "My parents . . . my *adoptive* parents were very good to me. I've always had everything I needed." A fat tear slid down her cheek. "I loved them very much. I just wanted you to know that." She paused and hiccuped. "I wanted you to know that you chose good people to raise me, and that you don't have to feel guilty anymore."

Fannie thought her heart would surely break at the confession and the sight of her daughter's tears. "I'm so proud of the way you've turned out, Mandy," she said, trying to talk around the lump in her throat. "So very proud. And I'm thankful for the wonderful couple who raised you. I wish I had known them."

The girl tried to talk, then choked on a sob. When Fannie reached for her, she went willingly into her arms. "I'm so glad I finally got the chance to meet you," she managed at last. "I just hate that they had to die."

Fannie held her tight as Mandy cried, deep heart-wrenching sobs that tore at her own soul and threatened to send her into a crying spree as well. How could she possibly send this child back now that she'd found her? "Me too, baby," she said. "Me too." She continued to hold her until the tears subsided.

The two stepped out the back door a moment later. The sun had come up but the sky was gauzy with a morning mist. Fannie turned to Mandy. "I guess you've figured out that Clay and I aren't really married."

Mandy nodded. "I think I was disappointed about that more than anything. I really like Clay."

They sat on a wooden seat that had been built around a large oak tree. "Well, he and I have been talking," Fannie said after a moment, "and we realize how much we want you to live with us, how much we want all of us to be a family. So we've decided to get married after all."

Mandy's eyes widened. "For real? When?"

"Today."

The girl shrieked and hugged her tight. "Can I be there?"

Fannie laughed. "We're counting on it."

They hugged again. "I knew the two of you were meant for each other," the girl said.

Fannie wished she felt as confident. "We'd like to face your aunt as man and wife," she said, "and see if there's any way possible to have you come back with us."

Mandy looked frightened. "What if she says no?"

"We have to take that chance. But we've already talked with a lawyer, and he feels this is the best way to go about it. Keep things friendly, as he says, then start the adoption process. If your aunt says positively no, then we'll be forced to battle it out in court. That'll take time, Mandy. I don't want you to get your hopes up that it's going to happen quickly."

"But you're my real mother," the girl said. "Why do you have to adopt me?"

"I gave up custody a long time ago, remember? I can't just snatch you back without concern for your present family. Your aunt may be difficult at times, but I'm willing to bet deep down she loves you."

"Way, way deep down," a sullen Mandy said. "I don't know why it has to be so confusing. Aren't I old enough to decide where I want to live?"

Fannie reached for her hand and squeezed it. "I don't want to tell you something that might not be right," she said, "and at this point we're trying to keep the lawyers out of it. We just have to approach your aunt and hope for the best. You'll have to trust us."

Fannie and Clay were married at three o'clock that afternoon at the town clerk's office with Mandy, Hyram, Gerta, Wilhemena, and the Dempsey sisters in attendance. Nobody had been shocked at the news since the newspaper had printed a notice of the marriage license that very day. Clay was dressed in a navy suit, and Fannie wore a sharp black-and-ivory single-breasted suit with a white straw hat adorned with a black gros-grain ribbon. Once they were pronounced man and wife and Clay had kissed her, there was much laughing and hand shaking and back slapping among the group.

Ernestine and Gussie, who'd both kept dainty white handkerchiefs pressed to their noses throughout the ceremony, could no longer hold the deluge of tears.

"I'm so happy for you," Wilhemena said, giving Fannie a firm hug. "I guess you know you snatched up the best catch in town," she said. "I may have to move my dress shop to a bigger town."

They arrived back at the house to find the chef had set up a buffet in the dining room, complete with a small wedding cake and champagne. Fannie turned to Hyram once he'd toasted the newly married couple. "How did you manage all this so fast?"

"I got to work the minute Clay told me you'd applied for the license." He wagged a finger in her face. "You shouldn't try to keep secrets from friends and relatives. Otherwise you miss out on all the wedding presents." He pointed to a stack of beautifully wrapped gifts. Beside them was a beige envelope with Clay's name on it. Hyram reached for it and handed it to his son. "This is for you."

Clay glanced at the neat lettering on the front, turned it over, saw that it was sealed, and slipped it into the pocket of his jacket. "Thank you," he said, knowing it was the deed to the property he'd always wanted. He was genuinely touched that his father had relinquished it, when in the past he would have held on to it whether he'd had any use for it or not. The man had changed from the tightfisted person he'd once been, and Clay couldn't help but marvel at that change. Those weren't the only changes, of course. He was kind and gentle and patient and genuinely seemed to care about those around him. He was all the things Clay had longed for in him as a child.

He stuck his hand out, and his father grabbed it, and they shook hands for the first time in years.

Finally, Hyram turned to Fannie. "And for you, young lady—" He reached into his pocket and brought out a set of keys, then handed them to her. "I decided what you needed most was a set of wheels. I worry about you in that old car of yours every time you go somewhere." He led the group out to the garage where they found a brand-new Ford Mustang wearing a gigantic red bow.

"Oh, Lord, I'm going to pass out," Fannie said, feeling her knees turn to rubber beneath her. She swayed once. An amused Clay reached out to steady her, and she didn't know which was making her more dizzy, the new car or his touch.

"Wow!" Mandy said, checking out the interior. "The seats are genuine leather, Mom."

She'd said it again. Mom. Fannie thought she'd died and gone to heaven.

"So what do you think, Mandy?" Hyram said, putting a hand on the girl's shoulder. "Aren't you just a little bit envious that everybody's getting presents?"

The girl shrugged. "I guess so," she said, but it was obvious she was so excited over Fannie's joy, she hadn't had time to think about it.

Mandy had no sooner gotten the words out of her mouth when the stablehand led a gentle-looking chestnut mare from around the back of the house. The girl looked at Hyram. "That's not for me," she said matter-of-factly, but there was a question in her bright eyes.

"I'm pretty certain it is," the older man replied, then thought about it for a few seconds. "Yep, I distinctly remember telling the man I wanted it for my granddaughter."

"Oh, wow," Mandy said, clearly dazed. She walked over to the horse slowly and touched the white spot over her muzzle as though she wanted to make sure the animal was real. The girl turned to the group of onlookers. "But what if I can't come back?"

"You'll be back," Hyram said confidently.

"When my son sets his mind to something, he seldom gives up until he gets it."

It was after five o'clock when Clay helped Fannie and Mandy into Hyram's Mercedes. Fannie had laughingly offered to lend him her car, but he'd insisted she should be the first to drive it. "I reckon I'm going to have to buy a family car," he told her as he pulled away. "I can't keep borrowing Dad's."

She nodded, but she was only half listening. She still couldn't believe they were really married, and she kept thinking about the envelope in his pocket. Why had he stashed it away so quickly and without comment, she wondered, then reminded herself it wasn't any of her business. Theirs wasn't a typical marriage, and she had no right to pry into his affairs. Clay was merely doing her a favor, marrying her in hopes of getting her daughter back. He'd even discussed with her what he'd be willing to pay if it didn't work out.

Her heart took a dive at the thought, and she realized how badly she wanted it to work. It *had* to work. Not only because she couldn't stand the thought of failing but because . . . well, because she loved him! That knowledge made her as light-headed as she'd been over the new car. She sneaked a glance in Clay's direction, taking in the handsome face she'd come to know so well, the same face that was so quick to smile, the face that gazed back at her so tenderly when they made love. But more importantly, she respected him. Even as far back as high school when he hadn't tried to get her into bed like the other boys.

It was late when they crossed the North Carolina border into Virginia and Clay began looking for a hotel. He selected a Hyatt, then asked for adjoining rooms and ordered a late supper from room service. Mandy hardly touched a thing on her plate.

"Nervous?" Clay asked.

The girl nodded. "You haven't met my aunt Rhea."

He squared his shoulders and puffed out his chest. "I'm pretty frightening myself, you know."

She shook her head sadly, but there was a smile in her green eyes. "Forget it, Clay. Mom's turned you into a big teddy bear."

Later, Fannie sat on the edge of the girl's bed until she fell asleep, knowing she was jittery at the prospect of facing the woman who'd taken over the job of raising her. One way or the other they'd work it out, she promised her daughter, then prayed she wouldn't be forced to break that promise. She had let Mandy down before, she refused to do it a second time. Besides, she couldn't imagine life without her.

When Fannie entered the room she shared with Clay a few minutes later, she found him in his pajama bottoms propped up on the bed watching television. His hair was damp, he'd obviously just stepped out of the shower. It sounded like a good idea to Fannie, who felt grungy after the long ride. She excused herself and didn't come out of the bathroom until she'd scrubbed from head to toe.

She emerged sometime later wearing the nightgown Wilhemena had loaned her. Her long hair was wet from having shampooed it. She reached for a comb and began to work the tangles out.

"Here, let me," Clay said, sitting up on the bed. He patted the spot in front of him. "I've always wanted to do that."

"It's not as much fun as it looks," she told him. Nevertheless, she handed him the wide-toothed comb and sat before him.

"How's the best way to do it?" he asked, noting there was quite a bit of hair to comb.

"Start at the ends and work your way up. It shouldn't be too bad, I used a big glob of conditioner."

He began combing. "So how's Mandy?"

"Not good," she said on a sigh. "But she finally fell asleep."

"And you?"

"I'm worried sick." She half turned. She caught the scent of soap and clean male flesh. "What if we don't get her? The poor kid is miserable living with that woman."

"All we can do is try our best. If all else fails, we go to court. One way or the other, you're going to have your daughter back. Try to be patient and trust me."

"I do trust you, Clay," she said softly, and meant it.

He was touched by her confession, and he knew it had not been easy for her to reach that point. He gazed at her for a long moment, thinking how lovely she looked in the gown, how tempting with the material falling against her breasts like a caress. He wouldn't have minded seeing her in something a little more provocative. He knew of a place in Savannah that sold sexy lingerie, and he decided he would have to visit it soon. He reached up and fingered the dainty lace neckline, and he thought he saw her nipples harden in response. "You know, we're going to have to buy you some clothes now."

Fannie chuckled softly and self-consciously as her skin prickled at his touch. All the man had to do was look at her and her body went crazy. "I know. Poor Wilhemena probably doesn't have a thing left to wear. I've just been so wrapped up in this other business . . ."

"How about when this is over, you and I take a honeymoon somewhere and do some shopping while we're at it." When she didn't say anything, he went on. "I can't have my wife borrowing clothes. What would folks think?"

She met his gaze. "I don't really feel like a wife," she said. "At least not yet."

He put the comb aside. "Then I'm obviously

not doing my duty as a husband." He pulled her back so that she was lying in his arms, and he kissed her deeply, running his big hands down the length of her, caressing and kneading her flesh. She felt small in his arms. Small and vulnerable. His *wife*. He had never felt so protective of a human being. He prodded her mouth open with his tongue and went inside. She surprised him by chasing his tongue back into his own mouth so she could explore.

After a while, kisses weren't enough. Clay pulled the gown over her head and ran his lips over her body. Their lovemaking was slow and thorough, taking Fannie to heights she'd never known. Clay watched her face closely as he stroked and kissed and nibbled, eager to learn where she was most sensitive, where he could give the most pleasure. He whispered sexy suggestions into her ear, and she responded with a passion that was yet unknown to her.

When at last they climaxed together, they drifted to sleep in each other's arms, their sweat-drenched bodies exhausted but completely sated. Fannie's last thought was of how much she loved him.

Rhea Turnbull's house was tucked between a line of row houses in an area near Capitol Hill, one of a small pocket of elegant neighborhoods left in what was fast becoming a ghetto. The house was a narrow three-story structure with a postage-stamp yard that barely accommodated a flower bed filled with pansies and herbs. Mandy told Clay and Fannie her aunt had bought the place thirty years earlier when the property was cheap. "She's a miser," the girl said. "Buys all her baked items at a thrift store where they mark it down after it's stale. I once saw her sneak out of the house in the middle of the night to steal a lamp shade out of a neighbor's trash beside the curb." She sighed. "I suppose it's not nice to talk about her like that."

"Perhaps she had it hard growing up," Fannie said, remembering how poverty had shaped her into being cautious with her money.

"Naw, she's loaded. She and my mother come from money."

Fannie could feel her legs shaking as they rang the doorbell and waited. The door was opened immediately by a tall, raw-boned woman with hair the color and texture of a Brillo pad. One vein-covered hand grasped a simple wooden cane. Her eyes, blue and alert, hardened perceptibly when they came to rest on Mandy.

"I hope you're proud of yourself, young lady," she said in an odd, fruity-textured voice. The girl seemed to shrink before her. "They've upped my blood pressure medication twice since you took off."

"May we come in?" Clay asked.

The woman nodded and backed away so they

could enter. She made her way to a chair that was draped in what looked like a bed sheet. "Please sit," she said, indicating the sofa which was also covered with a protective sheet.

Fannie glanced around at her surroundings as she made her way to the sofa with Clay and Mandy beside her. She felt suddenly claustrophobic in the narrow room with thick wool rugs and heavy brocade drapes and oversize furniture. She wondered if the woman ever removed the sheets or if she ever threw anything away. Pictures of every shape and size littered the walls and cluttered the numerous occasional tables, one or two so badly battered, she wondered if they'd been pulled from someone's garbage as well.

Clay, having decided to stand, was the first to speak. He motioned for Mandy to stand as well. "Mrs. Turnbull, I believe your niece has something to say to you."

Mandy stood slowly, glancing at Clay, then at her aunt. "I'm sorry for all the trouble I've caused, Aunt Rhea," she said. "I never meant to hurt you."

The older woman glanced away as though she were too angry to even look at her niece at the moment. She pressed her lips into two grim, unforgiving lines.

"I know how worried you must've been," Clay said gently. "My wife and I were horrified when we learned Mandy had run away. Especially after all you've done for her."

The woman regarded him. "Worried?" she cried. "I haven't slept in a week. The police tore her room apart looking for evidence of where she might have gone. Took me hours to put it back together. I'm not a young woman, you know." She paused and drew herself up, then turned her attention to Fannie. "So you're Mandy's real mother?" She looked her up and down as though trying to decide what to make of her.

"Yes ma'am," Fannie said, trying to remind herself to sit up straight. "Although I was happy beyond words to see my daughter again, I was truly distressed when I discovered the circumstances of her visit. She's very sorry for what she's done. I hope you can find it in your heart to forgive her. One day," she added when the woman's look didn't soften the least bit.

Clay crossed his arms. "We don't expect you to go easy on her, though," he said. "Mandy broke the law. She should be punished."

Rhea gave him her undivided attention. "What did you have in mind?"

"She should be grounded, of course. And nothing less than twenty-four-hour supervision," he added. "Otherwise, she'll run away again. Once a kid gets a taste of freedom, boom!" He hit a fist in an open palm. "Could be you're going to have to look into placement for her. Higher management, so to speak. That can be expensive as I'm sure you know, but Mandy is a stubborn, willful child, and unless someone takes a firm hand immediately, she's going to get worse."

"She's not an easy child," Fannie said, her own mouth grim. "I'm sure it has been hard for you."

The woman looked surprised but satisfied. "Well, I'm glad *somebody* finally shares my view of how the girl should be raised. My sister, God rest her soul, was too easy on her and look what happened."

"You're completely right," Fannie said. "You can't let children make their own decisions. That's what's wrong with our youth today. They have to be taught from an early age to toe the line."

Rhea studied Fannie closely. "Do you mind if I ask if you're a church-going woman, Mrs. Bodine?"

"Yes, ma'am. I'm a proud member of the Ebenezer Baptist Church. Thinking about joining the choir as a matter of fact."

"I'm a Methodist myself," Rhea said. "I understand the Baptists are fairly strict."

"Sometimes I feel they're not strict enough," she replied, drawing another look of surprise from the woman. "If you ask me, young girls have no business wearing short dresses and calling boys on the phone. I say it's high time we get back to the way it was, when men acted like gen-

tlemen and treated our young women like ladies."

"I couldn't agree with you more," Rhea said.
"By the way, have you had lunch? I can get my
housekeeper to put something together. I usually
take my nap at this time —"

"Did you hear that, Mandy?" Clay interrupted. "How is your poor aunt going to take a
well-needed rest when she has to watch you
twenty-four hours a day? How's she going to
know you're not sneaking out to meet some boy
while she naps?"

"Indeed!" Rhea said, literally glaring at her
niece.

Mandy gave her a sheepish look. "I'll try to
be good, Aunt Rhea," she said, kneeling before
the woman and putting her head in her lap. For
the first time the woman's face softened. She
raised a frail hand to the girl's head, seemed to
think better of it, and moved it away. "But sometimes I can't help it," Mandy went on. "I get
these urges to be bad and do all sorts of things.
Maybe you should send me to a home where I
can get help. I know it'll cost a lot of money, but
I can pay you back one day."

The woman was quiet for a moment as
though trying to calculate how much such a place
would cost, how long it would take for the girl to
repay her, and whether she'd live long enough to
recoup. Finally, she looked at Fannie, and there

was a pleading quality in her eyes. "I promised my sister I'd look after her."

Fannie took her hand and squeezed it. For all her faults, it was obvious the woman loved her niece and was doing her best. Perhaps she really didn't know how to show love. "I don't think your sister had any idea what she was asking."

The woman looked down at her niece and finally stroked her blond hair thoughtfully. When she looked up again, there was a hint of a smile on her lips. "You're very good," she said, her gaze going from Fannie to Clay. "You really had me going for a moment."

Fannie and Clay exchanged shocked glances. Mandy raised her head, eyes pleading with her aunt. "I want to go back with them, Aunt Rhea. I love you very much, and I still want to be able to see you, but—" She paused and looked at Fannie. "Now that I've found my real mother, I don't ever want to let her go."

"And how do you feel about that?" Rhea asked Fannie.

"I feel blessed to have a second chance."

They left two hours later, once Mandy had packed the last of her things and promised her aunt to write. The woman hugged her niece, eyes glistening with tears. "I hope I haven't let anyone down," she said.

"You've made us the happiest family in the world," Clay assured her.

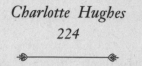

They drove as far as Wilmington, North Carolina, and checked into a bed and breakfast near the ocean. Fannie initiated their lovemaking that night, kissing Clay and stroking him as she'd only dreamed of doing before. Watching her through passion-glazed eyes as she straddled him, he cupped her hips with his palms and guided her as she impaled herself on his body. Fannie's heart swelled with love as she watched his handsome face contort with exquisite pleasure when he reached climax. She leaned forward and kissed him gently on the lips and wiped the sweat from his brow.

"I love you," she whispered. He gazed back in utter silence as though it were all too much to comprehend at one time.

They arrived home the following afternoon and told Hyram the good news.

"This calls for a celebration," the older man said, and sent Gerta to the kitchen for a bottle of champagne. He filled several champagne glasses, passed them around, then poured a tiny bit for Mandy. He winked at the girl when Fannie shot him a disapproving glance. "I'm a grandfather now," he told her. "It's my job to spoil her." He hugged the girl. "I can't tell you what it means to me to have all of you here. This big old house has sat empty too long."

Once Mandy had participated in the celebration for a bit, she excused herself to go check on her horse.

"Don't forget to change clothes first," Fannie said.

Mandy laughed. "You're beginning to sound like my mother."

"I *am* your mother," Fannie said, trying to sound stern despite the smile on her face. "And don't you ever forget it." She hugged her daughter tightly before the girl left the room, a definite bounce in her step.

"So how's married life treating you?" Hyram asked his son.

Clay glanced at Fannie and smiled, thinking about how they'd spent the previous night, making love until the wee hours of the morning. Her confession of love had stunned him but forced him to examine his own feelings more closely. He couldn't imagine life without her. "I can't complain," he said.

The man chuckled. "When I think what I had to dangle in front of you in order to get you to go along with this scheme and here you are grinning from ear to ear, happier than I've ever seen you look. Maybe I should ask for that property back. Hardly seems fair you should take it when I've done you such a favor."

Clay saw the smile fade from Fannie's face as his father continued to ramble on. "We'll talk about it later, babe," he said, winking at her.

Fannie felt a flush of heat on her cheeks.

"Would you please excuse me," she said, grabbing her purse and almost running from the room. "I think I need air."

Hyram looked distressed. "Did I say something wrong?"

Fannie made her way out the front door and around the back of the house where her old clunker was still parked. Tears stung her eyes and threatened to spill down her cheeks. She thought of taking Mandy with her but knew she needed this time alone and Mandy would be happier spending time with her horse. Besides, the girl didn't need to see her so upset. As she pulled out of the drive, she saw Clay hurrying out of the house, calling her name. She drove on.

Her house was the same, though it smelled mustier from being closed up. Fannie opened several windows, then made her way into the front room where her mother's hospital bed had sat for so long. She took a seat on the sagging sofa.

She felt like a fool.

She had fallen in love with a man who'd had to be bribed before he'd agree to pretend to be her husband. She had married a man who didn't love her in order to get her daughter back. What in the world had she been thinking? Who knew how long the union would last? What if it didn't? Wouldn't Mandy be better off with a strict aunt than she would with unstable parents?

Had she won her daughter back simply to fail again?

The thought shattered her.

No, she wouldn't fail Mandy this time. If they had to live in this house until she completed her education and found a better job then so be it. As long as they were together. One day she would be able to provide for her daughter as she wished. But she refused to live with a man who didn't love her, and she wouldn't allow herself to fall more deeply in love with him.

"Fannie?"

The voice startled her, and she cried out. Clay stepped through the doorway. "What are you doing here?" she demanded.

"I followed you. I knew you'd come here." He pulled a chair close and sat facing her.

He was so handsome, she almost couldn't stand it. Why had she allowed herself to fall for him? "I needed to be alone," she said.

"You're already thinking of calling it quits, aren't you?" he said. "I can see it on your face. Why are you so quick to give up on us?"

"What did your father have to give you in order to get you to pretend to be my husband?" she asked.

"A parcel of land I've always wanted. But I would have done it without the land, Fannie, just to be able to help you."

"I guess I'll never know that for sure, though, will I?"

"You said you trusted me." He was silent for a moment. "Do you want me to give it back? I will if that's what it takes to bring you home."

"You would?" She looked doubtful.

"The land means a lot to me, but it's not worth losing you and Mandy. Being with you has changed the way I feel about a lot of things. I thought it was my work making me unhappy and restless and bored. It wasn't my work, it was me. I had no substance in my life and nobody who really gave a damn about me. I had nobody I particularly cared about."

"You don't love me." It came out sounding like an accusation, but she couldn't help it. She would rather live in poverty than live with a man who didn't love her. At least with hard work she could build a better life for herself and her daughter. Clay, on the other hand, would learn to despise her after a while. Would he cheat on her as well? Would he eventually walk out?

His expression was pained. He could see the gears in her brain working overtime, comparing him to previous men she'd known. "How can you say I don't love you when you're the one who taught me what love was all about?" he insisted. "Because of you I was able to put aside the anger I had for my father and start a new relationship. Because of you, I look forward to getting up in the morning. I like myself better because of you."

He took her hands in his, and the sincere look on his face almost took her breath. "Fannie, don't throw away what we have. I may not be any good at saying the words, but if this isn't love I don't know what is. I'll get better at saying the words as time goes on. And you'll get better at trusting me."

She was genuinely touched by his confession. Still, she was uncertain. Her eyes stung with the threat of tears. "I'm scared, Clay. I promised myself I'd never depend on another person."

He raised her hands to his lips. "I know, babe. But I promise, no, I swear that I won't walk away from you. Neither will Mandy, she loves you too much. Of course, she'll go off to college one day, but you'll still have me and our other kids if we decide to have them."

Her eyes glistened. "I'd like a big family."

He smiled. "The more the merrier as far as I'm concerned. Once you get your education out of the way," he added sternly. "I'm going to see that you realize your dreams. And if it doesn't work out living where we are, I'll build us our own place."

She smiled through her tears. How could she not love this man when he was doing everything possible to make her happy? "Why are you being so agreeable?"

He smiled back. "Because I want you so much. Because I need you in my life." He kissed her lightly on the lips. "And because I'm crazy mad in love with you, Fannie Bodine."

That was good enough for her.

THE EDITOR'S CORNER

Along with May flowers come four terrific new LOVESWEPTs that will dazzle you with humor, excitement, and passion. Reading the best romances from the finest authors—what better way to enjoy the beauty and magic of spring?

Starting things off is the fabulous Mary Kay Mc-Comas with a love story that is the **TALK OF THE TOWN**, LOVESWEPT #738. Rosemary Wickum always finds some wonderful treasures in the refuse center, pieces perfect for her metal sculptures, but one thing she never goes looking for is a man! When recycling whiz Gary Albright begins pursuing her with shameless persistence, everyone in town starts rooting for romance. Once he nurses the embers of her passion back to life, he must convince his lady he'll always warm her heart. Irresistible characters and frisky humor make this latest Mary Kay story a tenderhearted treat—and proves that love can find us in the most unlikely places.

From the delightful Elaine Lakso comes another winner with **TASTING TROUBLE**, LOVESWEPT #739. Joshua Farrington doesn't think much of the Lakeview Restaurant's food or ambience, but its owner Liss Harding whets his interest and provokes him into a brash charade! Tempting her with strawberries, kissing her in the wine cellar, Josh coaxes her to renovate the building, update the menu —and lose herself in his arms. But once he confesses his identity, he has to persuade her he isn't the enemy. As delectable as chocolate, as intoxicating as fine wine, this wonderful romance from Elaine introduces charming, complex lovers whose dreams are more alike than they can imagine.

From the ever-popular Erica Spindler comes **SLOW HEAT**, LOVESWEPT #740. Jack Jacobs thrives on excitement, thrills to a challenge, and always plays to win, so when the sexy TV film critic is teamed with Jill Lansing, he expects fireworks! Five years before, they'd been wildly, recklessly in love, but he couldn't give her the promise she'd craved. Now she needs a hero, a man who'll share his soul at last. He is her destiny, her perfect partner in work and in bed, but can Jill make him understand he has to fight for what he wants—and that her love is worth fighting for? Steamy with innuendo, sparkling with wit, Erica's exhilarating battle of the sexes reunites a fiery pair of lovers—and casts an enchanting spell!

Rising star Maris Soule offers a hero who is full of **DARK TEMPTATION**, LOVESWEPT #741. Did special-effects genius Jason McLain really murder his wife, as the tabloids claimed? Valerie Wiggins approaches his spooky old house, hoping to convince him to help her make their Halloween charity event truly frightening. But when he opens the door, her heart races not with fright but sizzling arousal. Jason fears caring for Val will put her in danger, but maybe helping her face her demons will silence his own. Torn by doubts, burning with desire, can a man and a woman who'd first touched in darkness find themselves healed by the dawn? In a heartstopping novel of passion and suspense, Maris explores our deepest terrors and most poignant longings in the journey that transforms strangers into soulmates.

Happy reading!

With warmest wishes,

Beth de Guzman   Shauna Summers
Senior Editor   Associate Editor

P.S. Don't miss the women's novels coming your way in May: **DARK RIDER** from *The New York Times* bestselling author Iris Johansen is an electrifying tale of deadly and forbidden desire that sweeps from the exotic islands of a tropical paradise to the magnificent estates of Regency England; **LOVE STORM** by Susan Johnson, the bestselling mistress of the erotic historical romance, is the legendary, long out-of-print novel of tempestuous passion; **PROMISE ME MAGIC** by the extraordinary Patricia Camden is a "Once Upon a Time" historical romance of passion and adventure in the tradition of Laura Kinsale. And immediately following this page, look for a preview of the exciting romances from Bantam that are *available now!*

Don't miss these extraordinary books
by your favorite Bantam authors

On sale in March:

MISTRESS
by Amanda Quick

DANGEROUS TO KISS
by Elizabeth Thornton

LONG NIGHT MOON
by Theresa Weir

MISTRESS

Available in paperback by the *New York Times* bestselling author

AMANDA QUICK

With stories rife with wicked humor, daring intrigue, and heart-stopping passion, Amanda Quick has become a writer unmatched in the field of romantic fiction. Now the author of seventeen New York Times *bestselling novels offers another unforgettable tale as a proper spinster embarks on a delicious masquerade and a handsome earl finds himself tangling with the most exotic and captivating mistress London has ever known.*

DANGEROUS TO KISS
by Elizabeth Thornton

"A major, major talent . . . a genre superstar."
—*Rave Reviews*

*Handsome, kind, and unassuming, Mr. Gray seemed the
answer to Deborah Weyman's prayers. For once she accepted the position he offered, she would finally be safe from
the notorious Lord Kendal, a man she had good reason to
believe had murdered her former employer—and was now
after her. But there were certain things about Mr. Gray
that Deborah should have noticed: the breadth of his shoulders, the steel in his voice, the gleam in his uncommonly
blue eyes—things that might have warned her that Mr.
Gray was no savior but a very dangerous man. . . .*

"Study hall," said Deborah brightly, addressing
Mr. Gray, and all the girls groaned.

With a few muttered protests and a great deal of
snickering, the girls began to file out of the room.
Deborah assisted their progress by holding the door
for them, reminding them cheerfully that on the mor-
row they would be reviewing irregular French verbs
and she expected them to have mastered their conju-
gations. As the last girl slipped by her, Deborah shut
the door with a snap, then rested her back against it,
taking a moment or two to collect herself.

Suddenly aware that Mr. Gray had risen at their exit and was standing awkwardly by the window, she politely invited him to be seated. "You'll have a glass of sherry?" she inquired. At Miss Hare's, the guests were invariably treated to a glass of sherry when the ordeal of taking tea was over. At his nod, Deborah moved to the sideboard against the wall. The glasses and decanter were concealed behind a locked door, and she had to stoop to retrieve them from their hiding place.

As he seated himself, Gray's gaze wandered over the lush curves of her bottom. There was an appreciative glint in his eye. The thought that was going through his head was that Deborah Weyman bore no resemblance to the descriptions he had been given of her. Spinsterish? Straitlaced? Dull and uninteresting? That's what she wanted people to think. She had certainly dressed for the part with her high-necked, long-sleeved blue kerseymere and the unbiquitous white mobcap pulled down to cover her hair. An untrained eye would look no further. Unhappily for the lady, not only was he a trained observer, but he was also an acknowledged connoisseur of women. Advantage to him.

Since her attention was riveted on the two glasses of sherry on the tray she was carrying, he took the liberty of studying her at leisure. Her complexion was tinged with gray—powder, he presumed—in an attempt to add years and dignity to sculpted bones that accredited beauties of the *ton* would kill for. The shapeless gown served her no better than the gray face powder. She had the kind of figure that would look good in the current high-waisted diaphanous gauzes or in sackcloth and ashes. Soft, curvaceous, womanly. When she handed him his sherry, he kept his expression blank. Behind the wire-rimmed spectacles, her lustrous green eyes were framed by— he blinked and looked again. Damned if she had not snipped at her eyelashes to shorten them! Had the woman no vanity?

"I missed something, didn't I?" said Deborah. "That's why you are smiling that secret smile to yourself."

"Beg pardon?" Gray's thick veil of lashes lowered to diffuse the intentness of her look.

Deborah seated herself. "I missed something when Millicent offered you a cucumber sandwich. What was it?"

If he had the dressing of her, the first thing he would do was banish the mobcap. There wasn't a curl or stray tendril of hair to be seen. "A note."

"A note?"

"Mmm." Red hair or blond. It had to be one or the other. Unless she had dyed it, of course. He wouldn't put it past her. If this were a tavern and she were not a lady, he would offer her fifty, no, a hundred gold guineas if only she would remove that blasted cap.

"Are you saying that Millicent passed you a note?"

Her voice had returned to its prim and proper mode. He was beginning to understand why she had kept out of the public eye. She couldn't sustain a part.

"The note," Deborah reminded him gently.

"The note? Ah, yes, the note. It was in the cucumber sandwich." She was trying to suppress a smile, and her dimples fascinated him. No one had mentioned that she had dimples.

"Oh dear, I suppose I should show it to Miss Hare. That girl is incorrigible."

"I'm afraid that won't be possible."

"Why won't it?"

"On her way out, she snatched it back. I believe she ate it."

When she laughed, he relaxed against the back of his chair, well pleased with himself. That wary, watchful look that had hovered at the back of her eyes had completely dissipated. He was beginning to take her measure. The more he erased his masculinity, the more trustful she became. Unhappily for him, there was something about Deborah Weyman that stirred the softer side of his nature. Advantage to her.

Deborah sipped at her sherry, trying to contain her impatience. As her prospective employer, it was up to him to begin the interview. He lacked the social graces. She wasn't finding fault with him. On the contrary, his inexperience appealed to her. It made him seem awkward, boyish, harmless. Besides, she had enough social graces for the two of them.

"Miss Hare mentioned that you were seeking a governess for your young sister?" she said.

He was reluctant to get down to business. All too soon, things would change. That trustful look would be gone from her eyes, and Miss Weyman would never trust him again. Pity, but that was almost inevitable. Still, he wasn't going to make things difficult for her at this stage of the game. That would come later.

Deborah shifted restlessly. "You will wish to know

about references from former employers," she said, trying to lead him gently.

"References?" He relaxed a little more comfortably against the back of his chair. Smiling crookedly, he said, "Oh, Miss Hare explained your circumstances to me. Having resided in Ireland with your late husband for a goodly number of years, you allowed your acquaintance with former employers to lapse."

"That is correct."

"I quite understand. Besides, Miss Hare's recommendation carries more weight with me."

"Thank you." She'd got over the first hurdle. Really, it was as easy as taking sweetmeats from a babe. Mr. Gray was more gullible than she could have hoped. The thought shamed her, and her eyes slid away from his.

"Forgive me for asking," he said, "Miss Hare did not make this clear to me. She mentioned that in addition to teaching my sister the correct forms and addresses, you would also impart a little gloss. How do you propose to do that?"

There was an awkward pause, then Mr. Gray brought his glass to his lips and Deborah shrank involuntarily. She knew that she looked like the last person on earth who could impart gloss to anyone.

For a long, introspective moment, she stared at her clasped hands. Seeing that look, Gray asked quietly, "What is it? What have I said?" and leaning over, he drew one finger lightly across her wrist.

The touch of his finger on her bare skin sent a shock of awareness to all the pulse points in her body. She trembled, stammered, then fell silent. When she raised her eyes to his, she had herself well in hand. "I know what you are thinking," she said.

"Do you? I doubt it." He, too, had felt the shock of awareness as bare skin slid over bare skin. The pull on his senses astonished him.

His eyes were as soft as his smile. Disregarding both, she said earnestly, "You must understand, Mr. Gray, that governesses and schoolteachers are not paid to be fashionable. Indeed, employers have a decided preference for governesses who know their place. Servants wear livery. We governesses wear a livery of sorts, too. Well, you must have noticed that the schoolteachers at Miss Hare's are almost indistinguishable, one from the other."

"You are mistaken. I would know you anywhere."

LONG NIGHT MOON

by the spectacular

Theresa Weir

"Theresa Weir's writing is poignant, passionate and powerful . . . will capture the hearts of readers."
—*New York Times* bestselling author Jayne Ann Krentz

With her rare insight into the human heart, Theresa Weir creates tender, emotionally compelling, powerfully satsifying love stories. Now the author whom Romantic Times *praises as "a fresh and electrifying voice in romantic fiction," offers LONG NIGHT MOON, a novel that touches on the nationally important issue of domestic violence and affirms the power of love to heal the deepest sorrows.*

"I don't know what the hell—" His voice caught.

She was lying on her side, facing the window, clasped hands under her head, knees drawn up, eyes open wide, staring at nothing. And she was crying. Without making a sound.

Oh, Christ.

He was a man with no heart, no conscience, but suddenly he ached with an ache that was unbearable.

An ache that tightened his throat and stung his eyes. An ache he remembered but had never wanted to experience again.

For once in his life, he was at a total loss. He didn't speak. He didn't know what to say.

She pulled in a trembling breath. The sound seemed to fill the quiet of the room, adding weight to the ache in his chest. And then she spoke. Quietly, emotionlessly, her very lack of feeling a reflection of her measured control, of words doled out with utmost care.

"I thought I could be somebody else. At least for a little while."

He had no idea what to do, but he found himself pulling her into his arms. He held her, and he rocked her. He breathed in the scent of her. He stroked her hair, letting the satin tresses slide through his fingers.

Instinctively he knew that this was the real Sara Ivy. Not the socialite with her expensive gowns and jewels, not the hard woman who had snubbed him.

And the woman on the beach—she, too, was Sara Ivy. Defiant. Brave. Sexy.

That one drove him crazy.

But this one . . . this one broke his heart.

Time passed. The clock on the desk made its old familiar grinding sound.

Nine o'clock.

Sara lifted her head from his shoulder and let out a sigh. "I have to go."

Feeling strangely fragile, he let her slip out of his arms. Her body left a warm, invisible imprint on him.

She stood, gripping the blanket under her chin. "Don't watch me dress."

He had seen her naked body. He had a photo he stared at almost daily, a photo he'd lied to her about.

He turned. He walked toward the windows. With one finger, he pushed at the blinds. Metal popped, bent, making a triangle he could look through.

The full December moon. Low in the sky, blurry, as if a storm was moving in.

"Don't go," he said quietly, without turning around.

"I have to."

"Why?" He didn't want to think about her going back to Ivy.

She didn't say anything.

He made it a point to avoid intimate conversations, but suddenly he wanted her to talk to him, wanted her to explain things.

Rather than suffer the intrusive glare of a sixty-watt bulb, he opened the blinds, letting in just the right amount of light.

Behind him, he heard her move, heard the soft whisper of her shoes as she crossed the room.

He turned.

She was dressed and slipping into her coat. Her clothes seemed to have given her strength. Some of that cool, aloof control was back.

She went to the phone and called for a cab.

Anger—or was it fear—leaped in him. "What happens if you get home late?" he asked, his voice bordering on sarcasm. "Does he cut off your allowance?"

She silently considered him.

For the last several years, he'd prided himself on

the fact that he knew more about life than anybody. It was an arrogant assumption. Suddenly that truth was never more apparent. As she stared at him, the foundation of his self-assurance wobbled, and he experience a moment of doubt.

He had a sudden image of himself, standing next to a yawning precipice, ready to tumble headlong.

"Yes," she said with a smile that hinted at self-mockery.

He remembered that this was the woman who had tried to kill herself.

"He takes away my allowance."

They were talking around the problem, talking around what had just happened, or hadn't happened, between them.

"I don't get it," he said, frustration getting the best of him. He wanted solid answers. "Why did you come here? To spite him?" Then he had another thought, a thought that fit more with his original opinion of Sara Ivy. "Or was it to get yourself dirty, only to find you couldn't go through with it?"

She looked away, some of her newly regained composure slipping. "I . . . I, ah . . ." She swallowed. She pressed her lips together. "I was willing to make a trade," she said so softly he hardly heard her. "At least I thought I was." She shrugged her shoulders and let out a nervous little laugh. "Sex just doesn't seem to be a good means of barter for me." She clasped her hands together. "Perhaps if you'd wanted something else, anything else, it might have worked."

"What are you talking about?"

"Sex. That was your ultimatum, wasn't it?"

The room seemed to slant.

What had happened to him? How had he gotten so heartless?

There had been a time when he'd been more naive than Harley. There had been a time when he'd been a nice guy, too. And he'd been hurt. And he'd decided to get tough or be eaten alive. But this . . . Oh, God.

"I have to go."

Her words came to him through a thick haze.

"W-wait." Shaking, he grabbed a sweatshirt, then managed to stuff his feet into a pair of sneakers. "I'll walk you."

They made their way down the stairs, then down the hallway.

Outside, the moon was completely obliterated by snowflakes drifting earthward. They were huge—like tissue-paper cutouts, floating on the still air.

Sara's face was lifted to the night sky. "Snow." Her voice held the wonder of a child.

He watched as wet flakes kissed her cheeks, her hair, her eyelashes, melting against her skin. When she looked back at him, she was smiling. Not the self-mocking smile he'd seen earlier, but a soft, slow, real smile.

The wall he'd put up, the barrier he'd worked so hard and so diligently to build, crumbled.

And he knew, in that second, from that point on, that nothing would be the same.

He would never be able to look at the world with the same detachment, the same distance, the same lack of emotion.

They hadn't made love. Their bodies hadn't

joined, but *something* had happened. She had somehow, some way, touched his soul.

He, who had sworn never to love anyone again, watched her with a feeling of helplessness. He watched as snowflakes continued to fall on her face and hair and eyelashes.

A benediction.

He took one faltering step, then another.

Ever since the night on the beach, he'd known that he had to have her, possess her. But now everything had suddenly turned around.

Now he wanted more.

He stopped directly in front of her. Slowly, her face was drawn to his. Her smile faded. A question came into her eyes.

Slowly, carefully, he took her face in his hands, cupping her cold cheeks against his warm palms, watching as their breaths mingled. He lowered his head, watching as her eyes fluttered closed, as her face lifted to his.

His own eyes closed. And then there was just the softness of her lips.

Her hair slid over his wrist. Her hands came up around his neck.

He pulled her closer, bulky coat and all, his mouth moving over hers. Her lips parted, inviting his tongue. And when he slid it against hers, his heart pounded, his body throbbed.

A horn honked.

Reality.

A hand to her chin, he broke the kiss. Her eyelashes fluttered. She looked dazed, slightly disoriented.

"I'm sorry about what I said the night of Harley's party." His voice came out tight and strained and a little lost. "I sometimes say things I don't mean, just because . . . well, because I'm an ass." He brushed a finger across her bottom lip. "Come and see me anytime. We can play Monopoly. Or watch TV. Do you like to look at stars? I have lawn chairs set up on the roof of Shoot the Moon."

Honk.

She blinked, glanced over her shoulder, then back. "I have to go."

He wanted to extract a promise from her. He wanted her to tell him that she'd be back, that he would see her again. He loosened his hold and she slipped away.

She ran to the cab.

He followed, closing the door for her once she was inside. As the cab pulled away, he could see her watching him through the glass.

She lifted her hand in farewell.

Pathos. A word Harley had dug out of him, its meaning just now truly hitting home.

He lifted his own hand, the slow, lingering gesture mirroring hers.

How could one simple movement hurt so much? How could it be so bittersweet?

Fannie opened the medicine cabinet, hesitating a second before reaching for a bottle of aftershave. There was something decidedly intimate about going through a man's toiletries. She unscrewed the cap and raised it to her nose, and the scent made her shiver with awareness.

"Finding everything?"

Fannie jumped, almost dropping the bottle into the sink. She closed the bottle and nodded quickly. "Y-yes. I was just . . . I like smelling this stuff."

Clay looked amused. "What do you think of the way it smells?"

"Uh—very nice," she murmured.

"Yes, but you can't really tell by smelling it straight from the bottle." He leaned close. "Here, take a whiff. Tell me if you think I'm getting my money's worth."

Her stomach fluttered wildly when the tip of her nose grazed his hair-roughened jaw. She recognized the woodsy scent with just a hint of citrus, but this time blended with male flesh. The combination made her head spin.

"What do you think, Fannie?" Clay asked again, his breath warming her skin.

"Oh, yes," she said in a breathless gasp, "definitely getting your money's worth. And more . . ."

WHAT ARE *LOVESWEPT* ROMANCES?

They are stories of true romance and touching emotion. We believe those two very important ingredients are constants in our highly sensual and very believable stories in the LOVE-SWEPT line. Our goal is to give you, the reader, stories of consistently high quality that may sometimes make you laugh, sometimes make you cry, but are always fresh and creative and contain many delightful surprises within their pages.

Most romance fans read an enormous number of books. Those they truly love, they keep. Others may be traded with friends and soon forgotten. We hope that each LOVESWEPT romance will be a treasure—a "keeper." We will always try to publish

LOVE STORIES YOU'LL NEVER FORGET
BY AUTHORS YOU'LL ALWAYS REMEMBER

The Editors